GREENE FERNE FARM

RICHARD JEFFERIES

Petton Books

August 2009

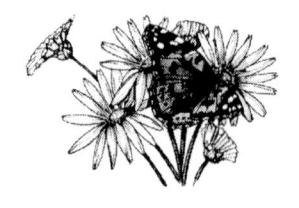

Greene Ferne Farm was first published in February 1880 by Smith, Elder & Co, Waterloo Place, London after appearing in serial form in *Time* magazine.

The book was dedicated to Jessie – Richard Jefferies' wife.

This new edition is published by Petton Books, The Richard Jefferies Society, Pear Tree Cottage, Longcot, Oxon SN7 7SS. Tel: 01793 783040.

August 2009

Web: http://richardjefferiessociety.co.uk

Printed by Cats Solutions Ltd., Swindon.

Introduction © George Miller 1993.

Cover image: oil painting of Chiseldon Church (featured in this novel) circa 1910 by Kate Tryon – on display at the Richard Jefferies Museum, Coate.

Back cover image: Richard Jefferies as a young man by Fanny Catherine Hall.

ISBN 978-0-9522813-6-8

Contents

		Page
Notes on the text		iv
Biographical note		v
Introduction		viii

GREENE FERNE FARM

CHAPTER I	'UP TO CHURCH'	1
CHAPTER II	THE SWEET NEW GRASS WITH FLOWERS'	12
CHAPTER III	THE NETHER MILLSTONE	23
CHAPTER IV	THE WOODEN BOTTLE	35
CHAPTER V	EVENING	46
CHAPTER VI	NIGHT	55
CHAPTER VII	DAWN	66
CHAPTER VIII	A-NUTTING	76
CHAPTER IX	GLEANING	87
CHAPTER X	A FRAY	100
CHAPTER XI	A FEAST – CONCLUSION	111
List of chief works by Richard Jefferies		121

Notes on the text

The original spelling and grammar have been retained from the first edition of *Greene Ferne Farm* apart from the correction of two printings errors and inconsistencies in the punctuation of dialect.

Acknowledgements

The Richard Jefferies Society extends its thanks to George Miller and Hugoe Matthews who allowed the reproduction of an extract from *Richard Jefferies: A Bibliographical Study* (Scolar Press: Aldershot, 1993) to be used as an introduction to this edition of the novel. Thanks also go to Jean Saunders for scanning and typesetting the book.

The Richard Jefferies Society

The Richard Jefferies Society is a Registered Charity (No. 1042838) with an international membership. Founded in 1950, it was set up to promote the appreciation and study of Richard Jefferies.

Further information can be obtained from the publishers.

Biographical note

Richard Jefferies was born on 6 November 1848 at Coate near Swindon in North Wiltshire, son of a small, struggling dairy farmer. His grandfather owned the chief mill and bakery in Swindon. Generations of Jefferies had been farmers in the isolated upland parish of Draycot Foliat on Chiseldon Plain since Elizabethan times. The mother's side of the family came from Painswick near Stroud and had strong connections with the London printing trade. The author's paternal and maternal grandfathers both worked for Richard Taylor of Red Lion Court off Fleet Street, a leading printer of scientific and natural history works. Between the ages of four and nine the boy was sent to live at Shanklin Villa, the Sydenham home of his Aunt Ellen and Uncle Thomas. Thomas Harrild was a letterpress printer with premises in Shoe Lane.

In 1866, after an irregular education, Jefferies joined the staff of the *North Wilts Herald,* a new Tory newspaper based in Swindon. He worked chiefly as a reporter but also published his first tales and short stories in its pages, as well as two local histories, of Malmesbury and of Swindon and its environs. He first came into wider prominence in 1872, year of the formation of the National Agricultural Labourers' Union under Joseph Arch, with three long letters on the condition of the Wiltshire labourer published in the columns of *The Times.* The letters attracted much attention and comment. During the mid-1870s Jefferies contributed articles on farming topics to such prestigious magazines as *Fraser's* and the *New Quarterly.* However, his chief ambition was to make his name as a writer of fiction and he published three novels (*The Scarlet Shawl* (1874), *Restless Human Hearts* (1875), and *World's End* (1877)) under the imprint of Tinsley Brothers, a frankly commercial and somewhat disreputable firm which had published Thomas Hardy's first three novels.

In 1877 Jefferies, now married to Jessie Baden, the daughter of a neighbouring farmer, and father of a small boy, moved to Tolworth near Surbiton to be closer to his Fleet Street editors while retaining a foothold in the country that was increasingly the source of his literary inspiration. The severance from his native county acted as a Proustian trigger, and on 4 January 1878 in the *Pall Mall Gazette* appeared the first of a series of 24 articles under the title "The Gamekeeper at Home", based on memories of Wiltshire and of "Benny" Haylock, keeper on the Burderop estate near Coate. The series attracted the attention of George Smith of Smith, Elder & Co, who published *The Gamekeeper at Home* in volume form in June. The book was widely and glowingly reviewed and ran through several editions. Jefferies followed it with others in a similar vein, *Wild Life in a Southern County* (1879), *The Amateur Poacher* (1879), *Hodge and His Masters* (1880), and *Round About a Great Estate* (1880), which the *Scrutiny* critic Q.D. Leavis called "one of the most delightful books in the English language". These works established Jefferies as the foremost natural history and country writer of his day. While living in Surbiton he also published a slight but charming pastoral novel, *Greene Ferne Farm* (1880); two children's books which have become classics, *Wood Magic* (1881) and *Bevis* (1882); and wrote the essays later collected under the title *Nature Near London*, about the remarkable variety and richness of wild life to be found in relatively close proximity to the capital.

Jefferies' health had never been strong and in December 1881 he fell ill of a fistula, probably tubercular in origin. He underwent four painful operations and the following year moved to West Brighton in the hope that the sea air would improve his health. Illness, coupled with the presence of the sea, which always held a powerful fascination for him, and the rediscovery of a chalk grassland landscape like that of his native Wiltshire, spurred him to write an autobiography of his inner life, a book about which he told the publisher C. J. Longman he had been meditating seventeen years. It was called *The Story of My Heart* and was a record of his mystical experiences from the time when, at

Biographical note

the age of eighteen, 'an inner and esoteric meaning' had begun to come to him 'from all the visible universe'. The book was a failure on publication (in 1883), but is regarded as the cornerstone of his work and a classic of English nature mysticism. William James in *The Varieties of Religious Experience* called it "Jefferies' wonderful mystic rhapsody".

His last four years were a heroic struggle against what Jefferies called the giants of Disease, Poverty and Despair, but he never ceased to write and dictated to his wife when he was too weak to hold a pen. During these years he produced much of his best work: the novels *The Dewy Morn* (1884), which Mrs Leavis described as 'one of the few real novels between *Wuthering Heights* and *Sons and Lovers*', *After London* (1885), which was greatly admired by William Morris, and *Amaryllis at the Fair* (1887), to make room for which on his shelf the critic Edward Garnett said he would turn out several highly-regarded novels by Thomas Hardy; and the essay collections *The Life of the Fields* (1884), *The Open Air* (1885) and *Field and Hedgerow* (1889), the last of which was edited by his widow and published posthumously. Of the later essays Jefferies' biographer Edward Thomas well said that 'both in their mingling of reflection and description, and in their abundant play of emotion, they stand by themselves and enlarge the boundaries of this typical form of English prose'. Aptly, one of Jefferies' last pieces was an introduction to a new edition of Gilbert White's *The Natural History of Selborne.* He died on 14 August 1887 at Goring-by-Sea, of tuberculosis and exhaustion, and was buried in Broadwater Cemetery, Worthing.

Introduction

Extract from *Richard Jefferies: A Bibliographical Study* by George Miller and Hugoe Matthews (Aldershot: Scolar Press, 1993), pp.197-202, with the kind permission of the authors.

The eleven chapters of *Greene Ferne Farm* appeared monthly in the magazine *Time* between April 1879 and February 1880, and the work was published in book form immediately on completion of its serialization. It was the first of Jefferies' novels published in which the scenes, characters and incidents are almost entirely of the countryside and derive from his intimate knowledge and experience of rural life. It may not, however, have been the first such novel that Jefferies had written. At least two earlier unpublished novels appear to have had a rural setting, and it is possible that *Greene Ferne Farm* was a revised version of one or other of these.

As early as 1868 Jefferies had written to his aunt describing a recently completed novel in which he had given up invented melodrama in favour of material drawn from his own experience. In this letter, dated 12th July, he says:

> I have taken great pains with it, and flatter myself that I have produced a tale of a very different class to those sensational stories I wrote some time ago. I have attempted to make my story lifelike by delineating character rather than sensational incidents. My characters are many of them drawn from life, and some of my incidents actually took place.[1]

The stories referred to are the wild tales of adventure and intrigue printed in the *North Wilts Herald* in 1866-7 and the

---

[1] Letter to Aunt Ellen from Coate, 12 July 1868, Manuscript 58822 vol XX, British Library.

Introduction

novel may have been *Only a Girl,* which he offered to Tinsley (and also Longman, according to Edward Thomas) in 1872. In a letter to Tinsley of September he describes it in terms applicable, in a general way, to *Greene Ferne Farm:*

> The scenery is a description of that found in this county, with every portion of which I have been familiar for many years. The characters are drawn from life, though so far disguised as to render too easy identification impossible. I have worked in many of the traditions of Wilts, endeavouring, in fact, in a humble manner to do for that county what Whyte Melville has done for Northampton and Miss Braddon for Yorkshire.[2]

But in another letter, dated May 1872, he says that the 'leading idea' of the novel is 'the delineation of a girl entirely unconventional, entirely unfettered by precedent, and in sentiment always true to herself.'[3] This suggests strong similarities with the heroines of *The Scarlet Shawl* and *Restless Human Hearts.*

The next rural novel was *In Summer Time,* written in 1875. Offering it to Tinsley, in October 1875, Jefferies says 'I think my new novel is the best thing I have ever written — it is full of the odd humours of the rustics I know so well, and has some original positions';[4] and to Bentley in April 1876: 'I think you will have found it original and perhaps not unamusing in the delineation of country scenes.'[5] Again the references to rustic humour and oddities suggest *Greene Ferne Farm,* but again also the term 'original' here (as 'unconventional', 'unfettered' etc. before), has connotations which link *In Summer Time* with the published early novels, and their adherence to the notion that the jaded novel reader of the day required extraordinary incidents and unorthodox moral standpoints. From these casual hints it seems unlikely, then, that either *Only a Girl* or *In*

---

[2] *The Eulogy of Richard Jefferies,* Walter Besant (London: Chatto & Windus, 1888), p.155. Includes extracts from letters and notebooks by Jefferies that are no longer extant.
[3] *ibid* p.154.
[4] Letter to Tinsley from Swindon, 9 October, Manuscript 58822 vol XX, British Library.
[5] Letter to Bentley & Sons from Sydenham, 22 April [1876], Manuscript 58822 vol XX, British Library.

Summer Time was a precursor of *Greene Ferne Farm* in any obvious or direct way. Further, as we shall see, Jefferies offered *Greene Ferne Farm* as well as *In Summer Time* to Bentley, the latter having been rejected after lengthy consideration. Even though over two years elapsed between the two submissions, Jefferies would surely not have offered what was substantially the same book a second time.

After discounting the possibility that *Greene Ferne Farm* was based on an earlier text, we are left with few clues as to its actual date of composition. There are no references to this title in the notebooks, and the untitled and incomplete sequence of manuscript pages relating to it are undated. [6] After *World's End,* written in the winter of 1875-6, Jefferies' next novel was *The Dewy Morn: A Summer Story,* which was completed by May 1877. He describes this, too, as a rural story full of rustic curiosities, but as 'totally different from my other novels'.[7] There may have been some justification for this claim, even though the 1877 version of *The Dewy Morn* would have borne little resemblance to the work finally published in 1884. In February the following year a significant entry occurs in the notebooks:

> Should be not more than three or at most four characters and entirely country and entirely pleasant as apart from revolting. Enlarge indeed as experience has shown the personal interest in one or two: in fact best if not more than three characters. Three at most.[8]

There are a number of other notes on fictional technique in the months that follow, one explicitly linked with the idea of revising *The Dewy Morn.* All of them show Jefferies' thoughts moving in the direction of deeper characterization, simplification of plot, concentration on the rural and elimination of the sensational; the direction, in other words, which was to produce *The Dewy Morn* of 1884 and

---

[6] Manuscript 58816 vol. XIV, British Library – untitled leaves of MS with nine leaves of notes and names relating to *Greene Ferne Farm.*
[7] Letter to W Tinsley, from Surbiton, 23 May, offering 'The Dewy Morn: A Summer Story'; private collection of letters.
[8] *The Nature Diaries and Note-books of Richard Jefferies* (London: Grey Walls Press Ltd, 1948), p.27.

Introduction

Amaryllis at the Fair. If *Greene Ferne Farm* were written in sequence, between the summer of 1877 and Spring of 1878 (and as we shall see there was a completed manuscript by September 1878) it would have been the first novel to reflect this transition. And indeed we find that although it does not entirely fit the new prescription (the plot is busier, the characters more numerous and slightly drawn) real structural and artistic change is evident. The book is essentially rural, with a spring-like freshness and clarity, a realistic idyll of the English countryside. It has 'the glamour – the magic of sunshine, of green things and calm waters'[9] which Jefferies was at the same point in time beginning to put into his non-fictional studies of natural history and rural life. Altogether the beginning of 1878, when the *Gamekeeper* sketches were first appearing, would have been a likely, and appropriate time, for *Greene Ferne Farm* to have been written.

The great success of *The Gamekeeper at Home* in 1878 transformed Jefferies' prospects as a writer, and he might easily have been expected then to have put behind him the failures and frustrations of his endeavours in fiction, just as earlier he had abandoned local history when his writings on agriculture and the countryside began to be widely accepted. Instead, while certainly not neglecting to follow up *The Gamekeeper* with projects of a similar kind, he seems also to have sought to use the advantages and confidence gained from it to revive his ambitions as a novelist. He turned to Frederick Greenwood, the architect of the *Gamekeeper's* success, for help in this also, but Greenwood was a reluctant sponsor of Jefferies' novels. It may well have been some specimen in the manner of his early fiction that occasioned Greenwood's warning to Jefferies against a false and flashy style, and when Greenwood was persuaded to act on Jefferies' behalf in this matter his recommendation falls somewhat short of being wholehearted:

---

[9] *Idler*, October 1898, vol. 13, p. 295. Oswald Crawfurd, 'Richard Jefferies: Field-Naturalist and Litteratteur'.

Permit me to introduce to you Mr. Richard Jefferies: the author of a series of papers which, after proving very successful as published in the *Pall Mall,* has been rapidly bought in book-form: I mean, *The Game-keeper at Home.* Mr. Jefferies has in MS. a novel of Country Life: this he wishes to offer to your attention, and though I have not read the story, I am strongly inclined to think it of the kind that deserves an hour's consideration at any rate.[10]

This, dated 23rd September 1878, is to George Bentley. Jefferies, of course, had had previous dealings with the firm of Bentley, notably in 1876 when he offered them *In Summer Time.* However he must have felt that George Bentley had either forgotten his earlier submissions, or had not taken a personal interest in them. On this occasion Bentley replied promptly, inviting Jefferies to send the novel, but with advance reservations about it apparent from the next letter we have, from Jefferies to Bentley, dated 30 September. Again the novel in question is not named, but turns out to be a version *of Greene Ferne Farm.*

> I am obliged by your attention and have the pleasure of forwarding the M.S. of my novel. You observe in your letter that 'to write the results of experience, and to conceive a work of imagination is not always given to the same person.' If the plot be subtracted I think I may say that nine tenths of my novel is the results of experience. Even the drunkard – Augustus Basset – is a sketch from life, and the original (now poor fellow deceased) was a member of a 'county' family which fell by degrees to the unhappy state described. The country folk are all also from life, the farmers, labourers etc. and if you wished I could even mention names in some cases: of course in confidence. The scenery is that of the Wiltshire Downs – from Ashdown (in Berks) to Salisbury Plain; they are my native hills and I know them well. The ancient dolmen which plays a part in the story actually exists. The *second* volume especially is drawn from nature: I have myself spent more than one summer night on the Downs, you would scarcely believe how beautiful the morning is just before the sun rises. I have tried to describe it: but the colours are not to be put on paper. I would rather like to take your attention to the second volume. The old farmer and miller

---

[10] *The Story of the Pall Mall Gazette,* J W Robertson Scott (London: Oxford University Press, 1950).

Introduction

Andrew Fisher was also a living character – he is not forgotten even now, and his house was ransacked when he died. Of course I have disguised the characters sufficiently that they should not be recognized too easily: but the substance is accurately portrayed. The scenes in the election – the canvassing of the farmers, and the specialist blacksmith are also real scenes – I have myself assisted in canvassing more than once: the difficulty is to get the farmer to come to the point, or to promise anything definitely. It is always 'Mebbe' with him.

In conclusion may I say that I should not object to slightly modify any part that may appear to you to require it, being always willing to accept advice from experience.[11]

The two-volume arrangement, very probably intended to correspond with two printed volumes, indicates that the novel was twice as long at this point as in its published form. The letter suggests what some of the extra material might have been. The character Augustus Basset would seem to have played a larger part. In the book he is described as 'a specimen of humanity not uncommonly seen on larger farms – the last relic of a good family, half bailiff, half hanger-on; half keeper, half poacher, and never wholly anything except intoxicated',[12] but he only crops up occasionally after this promising introduction. He may be connected with the 'specialist blacksmith' who doesn't appear at all in the book, but could be a relative of the blacksmith Ikey in *The Amateur Poacher* who specializes in rabbit poaching. Also in the published version there is no election. This part of the plot could have been transposed to *The Dewy Morn,* where a forthcoming election is spoken of and a rowdy meeting takes place, but no canvassing occurs.

Unfortunately we have no further documentary evidence until December the following year, 1879. Bentley's reasons for rejecting it, whether it was offered elsewhere (Jefferies offered a novel to Longman in 1878 – between June and

---

[11] Letter from Jefferies to George Bentley, from Surbiton, 30 September 1876. University of Illinois, Urbana.
[12] Page 17.

September, it appears from Besant's account;[13] this could well have been *Greene Ferne Farm,* why it was shortened, and the circumstances of its serialization in *Time* are all matters of conjecture. The background to the eventual publication in book form by Smith, Elder and Co. is also somewhat obscure.

In the case of *The Gamekeeper at Home* and *Wild Life in a Southern County,* Smith, Elder and Co. made the initial proposal of publication while serialization was still in progress in the *Pall Mall Gazette* – of which Frederick Greenwood, an old associate of George Smith's, was editor. Doubtless also their publication of *The Amateur Poacher* after its appearance in the *Pall Mall* was a matter of course. There seems, however, to have been no such understanding about works of Jefferies serialized in other journals, and in the case of the *Hodge* papers in the *Standard* and *Greene Ferne Farm* in *Time* the proposal seems to have come from him. George Smith wrote to Jefferies on 18 December 1879:

> I shall have the greatest pleasure in seeing you at any time when it may be convenient to you to favour me with a call... I have read some of your papers in the *Standard* and should be very glad to publish them in a collected form. I am doubtful as to the success of the novel for reasons which I shall explain when I have the pleasure of seeing you.[14]

The outcome of this was apparently an offer of £50 for the copyright of *Greene Ferne Farm,* a third of Jefferies' rate for a non-fiction work. He wrote on Christmas Day accepting this, but asking for an interest in any future editions. Smith wrote again on 29 December:

> I am much obliged to you for your letter of the 25th instant, which I should have answered sooner had I not been away from London.

---

[13] *The Eulogy of Richard Jefferies,* Walter Besant (London: Chatto & Windus, 1888), p.195.
[14] Letter to Jefferies from George Smith, London, 18 Dec 1879. Manuscript 58822 vol XX, British Library.

Introduction

If your novel should have a success beyond my expectation it will only be fair and reasonable that you should share in that success. I enclose a short agreement, which will I think carry out your suggestions, and a cheque for £50. If the agreement be in accord with your views, please sign and return one of the copies to me.

I will send your proofs in the course of a few days.[15]

The enclosed document is headed 'Memorandum of an Agreement', also dated 29th December 1879, between Richard Jefferies Esq. of Woodside, Surbiton, and Smith, Elder and Co., 15 Waterloo Place London, and stipulates:

> Mr. Jefferies having written a story entitled 'Greene Ferne Farm', assigns to Messrs. Smith, Elder and Co. the copyright of the story in consideration of their paying him the sum of £50...
>
> Smith Elder agree to print one thousand copies of the story as a first edition. And in the event of their publishing a second edition of the work, they agree to pay Mr. Jefferies a further sum of £50. Smith Elder further agree that if any subsequent edition or editions be published they will pay Mr. Jefferies a sum equal to ten per cent on the retail price of all copies of such subsequent editions sold by them. The second edition of Greene Ferne Farm is not to exceed one thousand copies.[16]

The instalments in *Time* were signed 'by the author of *The Gamekeeper at Home*', but the book was the first of the series published by Smith Elder to have Jefferies' name on the title page. It also had a dedication to the author's wife, Jessie, appropriate as the courtship of Geoffrey and Margaret in the story is based on Jefferies' memories of his own. Of the title itself, Rossabi notes that Green Fern was a meadow belonging to Jessie's father, Andrew Baden of Day House Farm.[17]

Greene Ferne Farm was published in the same format and a similar binding to *The Gamekeeper* and its successors. It looks very much like one of the same series, and

---

[15] Letter from G. Smith, London, 29 December 1879. Manuscript 58827 vol XXV, British Library.
[16] Publisher's agreement signed by Jefferies. Manuscript 58827 vol XXV, British Library.
[17] Introduction by Andrew Rossabi (p.11) to the 1986 edition of *Greene Ferne Farm*, Grafton Books.

was regarded as such in several of the reviews. The reviewers (none of whom recalls Jefferies' previous attempts in the art of fiction) are mildly approving of its merits as a novel, and just as enthusiastic about the descriptions of nature and landscape and rustic portrayals as they are in their comments on the companion volumes. Despite the publisher's misgivings, sales were good, though not as brisk as those of the three preceding non-fiction books, and the title was out of print within a year. In the circumstances it is not clear why a second edition did not appear. The fact that George Smith evidently kept a copy, which sometime after Jefferies' death he presented to his own wife with a romantic inscription, suggests that the reasons were purely commercial.

Greene Ferne Farm

Richard Jefferies

CHAPTER I

'UP TO CHURCH'

'FINE growing marning, you!'
'Ay, casualty weather, though!'
Ding – ding – dill! Dill – ding – dill!
This last was the cracked bell of the village church ringing 'to service.' The speakers were two farmers, who, after exchanging greeting, leant against the churchyard wall, and looked over, as they had done every fine-weather Sunday this thirty years. So regular was this pressure, that the moss which covered the coping-stones elsewhere was absent from the spot where they placed their arms. On the other side of the wall, and on somewhat lower ground, was a pigsty, beyond that a cow-yard, then a barn and some ricks. 'Casualty,' used in connection with weather, means uncertain. Mr. Hedges, the taller of the two men, stooped a good deal; he wore a suit of black, topped, however, by a billycock. Mr. Ruck, very big and burly, was shaped something like one of his own mangolds turned upside down: that is to say, as the glance ran over his figure, beginning at the head, it had to take in a swelling outline

1

as it proceeded lower. He was clad in a snowy-white smock-frock, breeches and gaiters, and glossy beaver hat.

This costume had a hieroglyphic meaning. The snowy smock-frock intimated that he had risen from lowly estate, and was proud of the fact. The breeches and gaiters gave him an air of respectable antiquity in itself equivalent to a certain standing. Finally the beaver hat – which everybody in the parish knew cost a guinea, and nothing less – bespoke the thousand pounds at the bank to which he so frequently alluded.

Dill – ding – ding! Ding – dill – dill!

The sweet spring air breathed softly; the warm sunshine fell on the old grey church, whose shadow slowly receded from the tombstones and low grassy mounds. The rounded ridge of the Downs rose high to the south – so near that the fleecy clouds sailing up were not visible till they slid suddenly into view over the summit. Tiny toy-like sheep, reduced in size by the distance were dotted here and there on the broad slope. Over the corn hard by, the larks sprang up and sang at so great a height that the motion of their wings could not be distinguished. The earth exhaled a perfume, there was music in the sky, a caress in the breeze. Far down in the vale a sheet of water glistened; beyond that the forest of trees and hedges became indistinct, and assumed a faint blue tint, extending like the sea, till heaven and earth mingled at the hazy horizon.

Humph – humph! The pigs were thrusting their noses into a heap of rubbish piled up against the wall, and covered with docks and nettles. Mr. Hedges leant a little farther over the coping, and with the end of his stick rubbed the back of the fattest, producing divers grunts of satisfaction. This operation seemed to give equal pleasure to the man and the animal.

'Thirteen score,' said Ruck sententiously, referring to the weight of the said pig.

'Mebbe a bit more, you' – two farmers could by no possibility agree on the weight of an animal. 'Folk never used to think nothing of a peg till a' were nigh on twenty score. But this generation be nice in bacon, and likes a wafer rasher as shrivels up dry without a lick of grease.'

'It be a spectacle to see the chaps in the Lunnon eating-houses pick over their plates,' said Ruck. 'Such a waste of good vittels!'

'There'll be a judgment on it some day.' The click of the double wicket-gates – double, to keep other people's sheep out and the rector's sheep in – now began to sound more frequently, as the congregation gathered by twos and threes, coming up the various footpaths that led across the fields. Very few entered the church – most hanging about and forming little groups as their acquaintances came up. The boys stole away from their gossiping parents, and got together where a projecting buttress and several high square tombs formed a recess and hid their proceedings. A broad sunken slab just there was level with the turf; the grass grew over at the edges. They had scraped away the moss that covered it; the inscription had long since disappeared, except the figure 7, a remnant of the date. Something like the chink of coppers on stone might have been heard now and then, when there was a lull in their chatter.

Dill – dill!

'Squire Thorpe got visitors, yent a'?' asked Hedges, perfectly well aware of the fact, but desirous of learning something else, and getting at it sideways, as country folk will.

'Aw; that tall fellow, Geoffrey Newton, and Val Browne, as have set up the training stables.'

'Warn he'll want some hay?' This was a leading question, and Hedges rubbed away at the pig to appear innocently unconcerned.

'I sold his trainer eighty ton o' clauver,' said Ruck. 'A' be a gentleman, every inch of un.'

'Stiffish price, you?'

'Five pound ten.'

'Whew!'

'Ay, ay; but it be five mile to cart it; and a nation bad road.'

'What's that long chap doing at Squire's? He 'as been to Australia.'

'A' be goin' to larn farming.'

'Larn farming!' Intense contempt.

'A' be down to Greene Ferne a' studying pretty often,' said Ruck, with a wink and a broad grin.

'Wimmen,' said Hedges, giving an extra hard scrape at the pig, who responded Humph – humph!

'Wimmen,' repeated Ruck still more emphatically.

'There be worse thengs about,' said a voice behind. It was the clerk, who, having put the rector's surplice ready, had slipped out for a minute into the churchyard to communicate a piece of news. He was a little shrivelled old fellow.

'Nash was allus a gay man,' said Ruck.

'So was his father afore un,' added Hedges.

'It runs in the family.'

'Summut in the blood, summut in the blood,' said Nash, not to appear to value the hereditary propensity too highly. 'Did ee never notice that shart men be a' most sure to get on with th' wimmen? I got summut to tell ee.'

'What be it?' from both listeners at once.

If the Athenians were eager for something new, those that dwell in the fields are ten times more so.

'You knows Mr. Valentine Browne as built the new stables?'

'Sartainly.'

'He have took my cottage for the trout-fishing.'

'Aw! You calls un Hollyocks, doan't ee?' said Ruck.

'A' bean't very far from Greene Ferne, be a'?' asked Hedges.

'Wimmen,' said the clerk meaningly. 'Tend upon it, it be the wimmen!'

'Lor, here um comes!' said Ruck.

Two young men walked quickly round the tower, coming from the other side, down the gravel path past the group, and opening the wicket-gate went out into the field. Nash bowed and scraped, Ruck lifted his beaver, but neither seemed to observe these attentions.

'It be the wimmen, and no mistake,' said Ruck. 'Thaay be gone to meet um. The Ferne folk be moast sure to come up thuck path this sunny day, 'stead of driving.'

'Marnin', shepherd,' said the clerk to a labouring man who had just entered the churchyard. 'I was afeared you'd be late. 'Spose you come from Upper Furlong. How's your voice?'

'Aw, featish [fairish]. I zucked a thrush's egg to clear un.'

'Arl right, Jabez; mind as you doan't zeng too fast. It be your fault, shepherd, it be your fault.'

For Jabez was the leader of the choir.

'Nash!' cried a stern voice; and the clerk jumped and tore his hat off at the sound. 'Catch those boys!'

It was Squire Thorpe, whose magisterial eye had at once detected the youthful gamblers behind the buttress. Nash rushed towards them; but they had scented the Squire's arrival, and dodged him round the big tombstones. Thorpe turned to the two farmers, who lifted their hats.

'Grass coming on nicely, Hedges,' said he. 'Ought to be a good hay year.'

The Squire was as fond of gossip as any man in the parish; but he was rather late that morning; for he had hardly taken his stand by the wall when the 'dill – dill' of the bell came to a sudden stop. The two gentlemen who had gone out into the field returned at a run.

'Ah, here you are!' said the Squire; and the three walked rapidly to the chancel door.

Ruck and Hedges, however, showed no signs of moving. A low hum arose from the hand-organ within; still they leant on the wall, deferring action to the last moment.

The sound of voices – the speakers clearly almost out of breath, but none the less talking – approached the wicket-gate, and three bonnets appeared above the wall there.

'It be the Greene Ferne folk,' said Hedges. 'Measter Newton and t'other chap was too much in a hurry.'

Three ladies – two young and one middle-aged – entered the churchyard. The taller of the two girls left the path, and ran to a tomb inclosed with low iron railings. She carried a whole armful of spring flowers, gathered in the meadows and copses *en route*, bluebells and cowslips chiefly, and threw them broadcast on the grave.

'Miss Margaret don't forget her feyther,' said Hedges.

The three, as they passed, nodded smilingly to the two farmers, and went into the church.

'May Fisher be allus down at the Estcourts',' said Ruck. 'S'pose her finds it dull up on the hills with the old man.'

'Mrs. Estcourt looks well,' said Hedges. 'Warn hur'll marry agen some day. Miss Margaret do dress a bit, you.'

'Nation gay. Hur be a upstanding girl, that Margaret Estcourt. A' got a thousand pound under the will.'

'And the Greene Ferne Farm when the widder goes.'

'Five hundred acres freehold, and them housen in to town.'

'A' be a featish-looking girl, you.'

'So be May Fisher; but a' bean't such a queen as t'other. Margaret walks as if the parish belonged to her.'

'If a' did, her would sell un, and buy a new bonnet. These yer wimmen!'

The sound of singing came from the open door under the tower hard by.

'Dall'd if it bean't "I will arise."'

'S'pose us had better go in.'

They walked to the tower-door. It was arched and low – so low that to enter it was necessary to stoop, and inside the pavement was a step beneath the level of the ground. Within stood the font, and by it some forms against the wall, on which the school children left their caps. There was a space behind the first pillar of the side aisle unoccupied by pews, being dark and not affording a view of the pulpit. Now it was possible to tell the rank of the congregation as they entered, by the length of time each kept his hat on after getting through the door. The shepherd or carter took off his hat the moment he set his hobnailed boot down on the stone flags with a clatter. The wheelwright, who had a little money and a house of his own, wore his hat till he got to the font. So did the ale-house keeper, who had the grace to come to church. So did the small farmers. Ruck, who could write a cheque for a thousand pounds, never removed his till he arrived at the step that led down to the side-aisle. Hedges, who was higher in the rank of society, inasmuch as he had been born in the purple of farming, kept his on till he reached the first pillar. One of the semi-gentlemen-farmers actually walked half-way to his pew-door wearing his hat, though the congregation were standing listening to Jabez and the choir get through the introductory chant.

Entering from the beautiful sunshine, the church gave the impression of a rather superior tomb. It struck chilly, as if the cold of the last five or six centuries had got into it and could not be driven out. Cold rose up from the tombs under the aisles – cold emanated from the walls, where slabs spoke of the dead – cold came down from the very roof. Whitewashed walls, whitewashed pillars – everything plain, bare, hard. The only colour to be seen was furnished by two small stained-glass windows, and the faded gilt and paint of the royal arms over the chancel; the lion and the unicorn in the middle, and the names of the churchwardens who reigned when it was put up on either side. The pews in the centre were modern; those in the side aisles high, like boxes. There might, perhaps, have been forty people in the church altogether – all crowded up towards the chancel: the back seats were quite empty. If a modest stranger went into such a back seat, and helped himself to the Prayer-book he might find there, the covers came off in his hand, and displayed a mass of sawdust-like borings thrown up by the grubs that had eaten their way right through the prayer for King William IV. A cheerless edifice – tomb-like; and yet there were some to whom it had grown very dear in the passage of years, and others to whom it was equally dear because of associations. So it was that this chilly, harsh, repellent place – squat rather than built on the edge of the hills – was beloved far more by some of the worshippers therein than those grand vaulted cathedrals whose vastness seems to remove them from human sympathy. But how marked the contrast between the sunshine, the blue sky, the song of birds, the soft warm air, the green leaf and bud without!

Squire Thorpe's pew of black oak occupied one entire side of the chancel; the choir and the barrel-organ were together, far down the side-aisle. From the raised dais of the chancel every member of the congregation could be discerned with ease. While the Rev. Basil Thorpe, cousin of the Squire, 'droned in the pulpit,' or rather reading-desk, the Squire, sitting, kneeling, or standing, surveyed with keen glance every nook and corner. This severe and continuous examination did not in the least interfere with his devotions. Such is the dual character of the mind, that he uttered the responses earnestly in his sonorous tones, and at the same moment noted the two wenches giggling with the ploughboy behind the pillar. His imagination followed the lesson and saw the patriarchal life on the plains of Chaldea, while his physical eye watched the grey-haired 'fore-father' in his blue smock-frock, who, leaning chin upon his ashen staff, traced the words with his horny finger on the book. The school children sat on forms placed endwise down the centre aisle. He saw one near the top stealthily produce an apple, and after taking a bite hand it to the next. All down the row it went, each nibbling in turn, and the final receiver putting the core in his pocket. Such innocent tricks did not annoy him in the least – his mind was broad enough to make allowances for the little weaknesses of human nature – the one thing that hurt him was the empty pews. He looked to see who was absent. He knew every inhabitant of the parish, and as it were checked them off mentally. It was a process he went through every Sunday with the same depressing result. The church was practically deserted: he hardly dared own to himself how small was the percentage that attended. Now the Squire felt no animosity against Bethel Chapel – he was candid enough to own that Basil was dull in the pulpit and somewhat mistaken in the tone of his intercourse with the poor. Still, to desert the church was as if a man turned his back on his own father, and preferred to sit at a stranger's hearth. He could not help associating it with that general divorce, as it were, of the people from authority, the general contempt for property and capital, the loss of respect for institutions of all kinds, that is so striking a feature of modern English life. Then his gaze fell on the group of three ladies in a high old-fashioned pew, and he marked Margaret's bonnet.

'Another,' was his thought – 'another since last week. But she is singularly handsome, and so like her poor father.' And his gaze grew gentle, noting the empty corner of the pew where the stalwart frame of his oldest friend had sat till darkness closed the eye of the boldest of riders and keenest of shots. Involuntarily he looked across at the marble tablet on the opposite wall of the chancel – set there at his own special wish – and read:

TO THE BELOVED MEMORY
OF
WARREN ESTCOURT.

The black lettering on the pure white marble grew dim; his eyes became misty. Then came the sorrowful, and yet assured, prayer:

'Make them to be numbered with Thy saints: in glory everlasting.'

Rude voices chanted it – voices used to the roaring of the wind in the trees and the hiss of the rain on the hill. Yet as they stood there and gave forth the old, old words that have been linked with human fate so many centuries, there came a meaning through the hoarse harsh notes.

A tear fell on the broad yellow page of the old Prayerbook the Squire held so closely to his face. This was why the low grey church was so dear to him; it was full of the past. Shadowy forms hid behind the pillars; faces looked down from the worm-eaten rafters; bright and yet quick-fading groups of other days appeared through the greenish-yellow panes of the windows.

'I am an old fool,' he said to himself. 'If these young fellows see me, they will laugh.'

But the young fellows by his side were otherwise engaged. They too had noted the extravagant bonnet; but their thoughts went no farther than the face beneath it. The old man thought of the father; the young men of the living daughter. But, indeed, Margaret Estcourt could not but be observed, standing so manifestly apart from, and yet among, that simple congregation. A single flower in a gloomy room will sometimes light it up as with a glory – the eye instantly rests upon it; a single violet will fill the place with perfume. She was the violet in that ancient building. Yet there was nothing extraordinary about her – no marvellous hyacinthine or golden tresses, no burning eye flashing with southern passion. She was simply very near the ideal of a fair young English girl, in the full glow of youth and with all its exquisite bloom. Perhaps at the first glance the beautiful pose of the tall and graceful figure seemed her most distinctive characteristic. The slight form of May Fisher brought her still more into relief.

So to the young men in the chancel pew the old grey church began to grow very dear, and the first part of the service slipped by speedily, despite Basil's droning. Then the choir gave out a hymn with all their might, sturdily drowning the organ, stimulated to an extra effort by the presence of visitors in the Squire's pew. Jabez the shepherd sang like a giant refreshed with wine, and got through four verses magnificently. But in the triumph of the moment he forgot the clerk's warning not to 'zeng too fast.' The verse finished with the word 'Jacob:' Jabez unfortunately got a little in advance of the time, and desperately struggling to lengthen it out, an ale-house chorus slipped from his tongue: 'Ja-aa-fol-de-rol-cob!'

When Basil went up into the pulpit the Squire quietly folded a silk handkerchief as a cushion to protect the back of his head from the hard oak of the pew, and slumbered peacefully till at the Rector's 'Fifthly, and in conclusion,' the stir of relief that ran through the congregation awoke him, as it usually did. Thorpe waited in the churchyard for Mrs. Estcourt, and walked with her as far as the wicket-gate, his own carriage waiting at the road entrance. There at the wicket the group paused a moment on the edge of the green fields. The sweetness of the air coming from the Downs, after the close and yet chilly atmosphere of the church, was in itself an exquisite pleasure. The larks still sang, the sun still shone, and the clouds came over the hill. Yet there was something more beautiful still in the mantling colour of Margaret's soft cheek. Youth and love – youth and love and May-time.

Cuckoo – cuckoo! from the bird on the elm below the hill.

'O, look!' said Mrs. Estcourt, suddenly, in some alarm, yet laughing. 'My poor shepherd' – for Jabez worked for her. Wildly he fled over grassy grave and tombstone, chased by a mob of smock-frocks and boys yelling 'Fol-de-rol-cob!' at his heels, till, reaching the wall, he leaped, hitched his toe in the coping, and fell prone among the docks and nettles and pigs.

The Squire laughed heartily. By-and-by, as he leaned back in his carriage, the thought came into his mind that this was human life in little. First, pathos in the memory of his old friend; next, love – for he shrewdly suspected Geoffrey and Val – and beside that love the grim tomb and sad low mound; finally, the grotesque. Wherefore the old monks, seeing that all life came to the church in their day, carved fantastic faces on the gargoyles grinning down, sneering and mocking at it. And even sweet young love brought its regret. 'For,' thought he to himself, as he narrowly scanned the faces of the young men sitting opposite, 'I fancy I detect a coldness and distance already between these boys, who used to be more than brothers. Margaret has come between them.'

CHAPTER II

'THE SWEET NEW GRASS WITH FLOWERS'

BAA — BAA! A long-drawn pettish bleating that sometimes sounded absurdly like the 'Ma – ma!' of a spoilt child. The lambs gambolled in the genial sunshine over the daisies; the ewes, arrived at the age of common sense, fed steadily on the young sweet grass, and did not notice the flowers.
Geoffrey Newton looked at them from the other side of the hedge, where indeed he had no business to be. He had carelessly wandered in a day-dream from the footpath, and was now in the midst of mowing-grass, to walk in which is against the unwritten laws of country life, because when trampled down it is difficult to mow. Yet there is a great pleasure in pushing through it, tall grasses and bennets and sorrel stems reaching to the knee – the very dogs delight in it. See a spaniel just let loose; how he circles round, plunging over it! – visible as he bounds up, lost to sight next moment in the matted mass; the higher it is the more he likes it.

Baa – maa!

'For how many thousand years have the lambs been happy in the spring-tide?' thought Geoffrey. 'And yet it is said that the world is growing old! Nature is always young. Earth was never younger than she is to-day. Goethe was right there:

> Thy works sublime are now as bright
> As on creation's day they rose.

If we could only somehow translate that eternal youth into our own lives – if! The dew still lingers here in the shade. How slumberous it is even in the morning! Unseen lotus-flowers bloom in the spring, and the odour makes us drowsy.'

His eyelids fell as he walked on, and his slow steps led him whither they would.

When a thoughtful man feels an overpowering love – a great passion rising within him – his ideal often becomes a kind of judge. All the creed of life that has grown up in the mind is passed in review: will the half-formed scepticism, the firm dogma, the theory, stand before the new light thrown upon them by the love that is in itself a faith?

So he dreamed of Margaret, and saw and did not see the beauty around him. His feet, sinking into the soft green carpet, were dusted over with the yellow pollen of the buttercups. The young shoot of the bramble projecting from the bush caught at his sleeve; but the weak tender prickles, not yet hardened into thorns, gave way, and did not hold. Slender oval leaves on a drooping-willow bough lightly brushed without awaking him. The thrush on her nest sat still, seeing with the intuition of a wild creature that no harm threatened her. Finches sang on the boughs above, and scarcely moved as he passed under.

'Crake – crake!' from the thickest of the grass where the bird crept concealed. Butterflies fluttered from flower to flower in their curious sidelong way. Every branch and bush and blade of grass – the air above where the swallow floated, the furrow in the earth where the mice ran – all instinct with life; the glamour of the sunshine filling the field with a magic spell.

A little brook slipped away without a sound past the tall green rushes and the water-plantains and the grey chequered grass that lifts its spear-like points in moist places; a swift shallow streamlet winding through the meadow, its clear surface almost flush with the sward. Now running water draws a dreamer; so he followed it across the mead, past the footpath and the stepping-stone that had sunk into the stream: past the dark-green bunches of the marsh marigolds, whose broad golden petals open under the harsh winds of early spring, and not far from the peewit's nest; for she rose and flew round him, calling plaintively, her pure white breast almost within reach, till finding that her treasure was unheeded, she slowly dropped behind: past the dog-violets, blue but not sweet, that looked up more boldly than their forerunners, whose modest heads had scarce appeared above the dead leaves on the bank. Yonder the roan cattle were feeding; and in the midst stood an ancient, gnarled, and many-twisted hawthorn, whose bark had become as iron under the fierce heats and fiercer storms of years; yet its branches were green, and crowned with the may-white virgin may-bloom scenting the air – and under its shadow a young heifer meditated. Past hollow willows, till presently the turf beneath grew soft and yielding as velvet, his foot sinking into the pile of the moss, and the shade of trees fell on him, where the bank of the brook became steep, and low down in its bed it rushed into the wood.

After awhile oak and elm gave place to black and gloomy firs that hung over and darkened the water. Large flecks of grey lichen clung to them, and from above a red squirrel peered down. Here the thick branches forced his steps aside from the stream, and out among the ash-poles where the wood-pigeons built their nests, and in the strength of their love looked down upon him fearlessly from their feeble platforms of twigs. Under an ash-stole he saw a rare plant growing, and stooped and went on his knees to reach it, and so pushed aside the thick boughs, and, as it were, looked through a screen, and his heart gave a great bound.

There was a narrow space clear of wood, where a green footpath little used went by, and a large, gnarled, crooked-grown ash-stole opposite, forming a natural arm-chair, well lined with soft dry moss, and canopied overhead with leafy branches, drooping woodbine, and climbing briar, whose roses would soon bloom. The brake fern, young yet and tender, rose up and gave itself for her footstool – for Margaret sat there, leaning back luxuriously in her woodland throne. He thought she must have heard the rustling of the boughs he had parted, and kept still as an Indian hunter, holding his breath for fear lest she should see him thus spying. A minute passed, and there was no motion; then he saw that her right arm hung down listlessly – that the head leaned a little to one side, the face rather away from him – that her hat had evidently dropped from her hand, and an open book had fallen at her feet. She was slumbering.

His chest pressed on the green fern, bluebells hung over his feet.

'Coo-coo-oo!' the dove with burnished neck called gently to his mate, sitting on the ivied tree.

'Jug-jug-jug!' sang the nightingale hard by in the hawthorn – the nightingale that by night is sad, but whose heart is full of joy in the morning. The goldfinches swept by overhead with a gleam of colour from their wings, coquetting on their way to the apple-trees.

The sun looked on the world with glorious eye.

A ray, warm, but yet not fiercely so, fell aslant between the leaves of the great oak boughs above, and lit up one delicate ear – small, white, with pink within, as in the shell the cameo-cutter graves with his tool; or rather, pink like the apple-bloom, that loveliest of flowers – for as a blossom it peeped forth beneath her brown wavy hair. Her lips were slightly parted: 'Thy teeth are like a flock of sheep that are even shorn, which came up from the washing.' For their backs are level and white, and glisten with the water. The highly-arched eyebrows did not meet above the straight nose, but left a space there. In some old magic-book he had read that this space was the peculiar precinct of the Queen of Love. A briar had jealously snatched at the loose sleeve of the right arm, which hung down, baring the wrist – a round, soft, white arm, veined with blue, an exquisite polish on the skin. The fingers were long and slightly rosy; from them a few flowers had dropped on the open page of the book.

So still was he that a weasel came along the green path, his neck erect like a snake in the grass, stopped, looked him straight in the eyes, and went by without fear. He gazed, rapt in the devotion of the artist, till a sense came over him like that feeling which the Greeks embodied in the punishment that fell on those who looked unbidden upon the Immortals. It was the strength and the perfect purity of the passion that held him there that also impelled him to withdraw. Slowly he worked his way backwards noiselessly, till, sufficiently far away, he rose to his feet, and hesitated.

Then he made a detour, and stepped into the green footpath thirty or forty yards distant from her throne, and began to make a noise as he approached her. He rustled the fern with his foot; he seized a branch and forcibly snapped it, causing a sharp crack. A woodpecker, startled, flew off with a discordant 'Yuckle!' the dove ceased to coo; the brown nightingale was silent, and sought a distant hazel-thicket. He lifted his voice and sang – he had a naturally fine voice – a verse of the dear old ballad, his favourite:

> 'If she be dead, then take my horse,
> My saddle and bridle also;
> For I will unto some far country,
> Where no man shall me know.'

Off came his hat – she had risen and faced him, blushing faintly. Her deep grey eyes looked down, and the long eyelashes drooped over them, as she held out her hand.

'I was coming to Greene Ferne' said he, 'and lost my way in the copse.'

'You must have gone a long way round.'

'Never mind – my instinct guided me right;' then, seeing that the meaning he expressed behind the words still further confused her, he added, 'It was quite accidental.'

Now Margaret had roamed out into the fields under the influence of a dawning feeling, which as yet she hardly admitted to herself, but which seemed to desire solitude.

And he had surprised her dreaming of him. So she walked silently before him – the path was narrow – glad that he could not see her face, leading the way to the farm. Outside the copse he came to her side, ruthlessly trampling down the mowing-grass again. There was a slight movement among the cattle in the next field, and they saw several persons approaching. They were May Fisher, Valentine Browne, the Rev. Felix St. Bees, and a tall, ill-dressed, shambling fellow hanging in the rear, whom they called Augustus. Instantly the thought occurred to Margaret that they would at once conclude her meeting with Geoffrey was prearranged.

'We were coming to find you,' said May. 'We have lost you all the morning.'

Valentine looked sharply from one to the other, jealously suspicious, and barely acknowledged Geof's greeting. So Felix and he fell into the rear, Margaret went on with May, and Valentine accompanied them.

St. Bees, a little quick-mannered man, was one of that noble band who may be said to give their lives for others. With ample private means, he accepted and remained in the curacy of Kingsbury, the stipend paid for which was nominal. Many of the workmen in the town walked in daily from the villages, and Felix visited them at their homes; frequently preaching, too, for Basil Thorpe at Millbourne, the village of which Greene Ferne was a tithing or small hamlet. He and Newton were old friends – his own love for May no secret. Augustus Basset was a specimen of humanity not uncommonly seen on large farms – the last stray relic of a good family, half bailiff, half hanger-on, half keeper, half poacher, and never wholly anything except intoxicated. An old soldier (he had served as a trooper in the Guards), his appetite for tobacco was insatiable, and as he walked he mumbled to himself, louder and louder, till by-and-by gaining courage he asked Geoffrey for a cigar. Newton at once handed him his case, when Mrs. Estcourt, coming out from the house, and detecting this piece of begging, told him to go and see about engaging some mowers, who would soon be required.

'There ain't no mowers to be got,' grumbled Augustus, as he shambled off. 'If you don't look out, you won't have a man on the farm; there'll be a strike. Just as if a man couldn't be trusted in the cellar, her keeps the key in her pocket!' Intense disgust!

They had some lunch at the farm; then Geoffrey and Valentine, feeling that they had no excuse for remaining longer, left together. But three fields distant, Valentine remarked that he must go down and see to his cottage, simply an excuse to part company. So each pursued his way alone.

Passing into the highway road that ran through the hamlet, Valentine, as he went by the Spotted Cow, a small wayside inn, saw Ruck and Hedges sitting with others outside, enjoying a pipe and gossip under the elm from which the sign was hung. On the rude table before them stood some mugs. Valentine beckoned to Ruck, who came.

'Have you sent up the clover?'

'Eez, eez.'

'And the oats?'

'Thaay be goin' up this arternoon, sir.'

'My trainer said your last hay was not so good.'

'Did a'? Then he doan't knaw good clauver when a' sees it. This be vine tackle, I can tell ee.'

'Well, I hope it is. Good day.'

'A' be terrable sharp about his osses,' said the old man, when he got back to his seat; 'but I thenks zumtimes as thur be volk that be sharper than he.'

'Who do ee mean?' asked his crony, Farmer Hedges.

'Aw, we shall zee. I've got half a mind to tell un; but he won't take no notiss of such as we.'

'Not a mossel of use,' said Hedges sententiously. 'These yer quality be such a akkerd lot;' and he knocked the ashes out of his pipe on the iron-bound edge of the trestle-table. The object of this armour was to prevent the labourers sticking their billhooks into it when they called for a quart, for hedge-cutters are apt to strike their tools into the nearest piece of wood when they want their hands free. Having filled the pipe again, and finding he had no match, he stepped into the inn-kitchen to light it at the fire, and instantly noticed a large red-hot nail in a log of burning wood.

'Missis, missis!' The landlady came running. 'Look ee thur – thur's a crooked nail in thuck log. Draw un out – doan't ee waste un. Nails be amazin' useful thengs.'

'Zo um be,' said Farmer Ruck. 'Volk used to save um. I knowed them as had a gallon measure full of hoss-stubs: thaay be the toughest iron, and makes the vinest gun-barrels.'

'Them cut nails be as rotten as matchwood,' said Bill the 'wunt-catcher,' i.e. mole-catcher, throwing down his wooden traps. 'Time o' day to ee, missus;' nodding to her over the mug, and meaning good health. 'The vinest gun as ever you seed wur thuck long un up to Warren. Mebbe you minds Kippur Mathew?'

'I minds un,' said Farmer Ruck.

'Thuck gun would kill vour chain. Thur wur a hole in the barrel as yer med put yer vinger in. Mathew, he squints along at the geame, and I holds a dock-leaf [18] auver this yer hole, and he lets vly, and kills half a score o' quests' [woodpigeons].

'A' wur a chap to fiddle,' said Hedges. 'A' made hisself a fiddle out o' thuck maple as growed in Little Furlong hedge. Hulloa, Pistol-legs!'

This was addressed to an aged man who had crawled up on two sticks. His legs, bent outwards – curved like the butt of a pistol – had obtained him this nickname.

'Nation dry weather,' said the ancient, lifting his head with some difficulty. 'Gie me a drap.'

A labourer leaning against the elm handed him his quart.

'Ay, ay; thur bean't no such ale as thur used to be;' – after he had taken his fill.

'I say, Gaffer,' said another fellow, a carter, who had left his horses by the drinking-trough – 'I say, Gaffer Pistol-legs, how old bist thee?'

---

[18] This expedient of the dock-leaf over a crack in the barrel was actually put in practice.

'Aw,' said the patriarch, shaking his head, 'I be amazin' old, I be. I be vourscore and five yaar come Christmas.'
'Warn you minds a main deal?'
'I minds when the new water-wheel wur put in Fisher's mill.'
'When wur thuck?'
'Aw, about dreescore year ago.'
'Anything else, Gaffer?'
'Eez; I minds when your grandfeyther wur put in the stocks.'
'Ha, ha! and after all your 'sperience, Pistol-legs, what do ee think be the best theng of all?' said Hedges.
'Aw,' said the ancient, picking up his sticks, and delivering his philosophy of the *summum bonum* with intense gusto. 'The vinest theng of all be a horn o' ale and a lardy-cake!'

'S'pose I must be gettin' on,' said Hedges presently, and stuffing some hay, which had worked out, into his boot again – for he used hay instead of stockings – he got up, and with Ruck walked down the road.

'A pair of skinvlints,' said the wunt-catcher, looking after them. 'One night up to West Farm they was settling a dealing job between um. Zo thur wur a fire, for the snow wur on the ground. Ruck he says, "A fire be a terrable waste, you. Let's put he out." Zo they doughted the fire, and both got their feet thegither in a zack.'

By a stile the two farmers thus careful of their fuel were gossiping before parting. 'Tell ee what,' said Ruck, in a mysterious tone; 'this here dark hoss as Val Browne be training for the autumn yent no go. He doan't know, and it bean't no good to tell un – these yer quality be so uppish. But thur be a screw loose somewhere; his trainer be a bad un. Doan't ee put a crownd on un.'

'Aw, to be zure,' said Hedges. 'That there Guss Basset will catch it zum ov these yer days. Squire's kippur says a' be allus in th' wood a-poaching.'

Then they parted, and a curious sight it was. First one would go a few paces, and then stop and talk, and presently come back to the stile again. Then both would walk away, and turn when ten yards distant and gossip, till by degrees they met at the stile once more. Not till this process had been repeated at least five times did they finally separate.

Later in the afternoon Geoffrey strolled out from Thorpe Hall into the park, and sat down under the shade of a huge beech tree, on the verge of the wood, whence he could just see the roof of Greene Ferne in the meadows far below. There he reclined and pondered – 'Where thy treasure is, there will thy heart be also.'

'Tu-whit-tu-what!' came the sound of a scythe being sharpened in a mead below.

Presently he became aware of a heavy footstep approaching; the massive trunk of the beech hid him from sight. It was a milker going to the pen. Geoffrey heard him turn his bucket bottom upwards and sit down upon it.

'Danged ef it bean't vour, I knaws,' he muttered. 'The sun's over Kingsbury steeple. Wurs Rause (Rose): bean't hur a-coming?' Then he began to sing, as milkers do to their cows.

'Thee's got a voice like a wood-pigeon,' said a woman whom Geoffrey heard get over the gate at the corner of the wood. 'Thee mumbles, Tummas, like a dumble-dore in a pitcher!'

Geoffrey peeped round the tree, and saw a stout girl in short petticoats, corduroy gaiters, brown hair, and dark eyes.

Tummas: Doan't thee say nought: I hearn thee in church like a charm o' starlings.

Rause: Thee go on to milking.

Tummas: I wunt. Come and zet on my knee.

Rause: I'll zee thee in the pond vust with thee gurt vetlocks uppermost.

Tummas: Aw, wooll ee?

Rause: Eez, ee wooll.

Tummas: Bist a-goin to haymaking to year?

Rause: Eez, in the Voremeads to-morrer.

Tummas: Zum on um means to gie out and ax for a crownd more. Gwain to strike, doan't ee zee?

Rause: A passel o' fools.

Tummas: Arl on um ull join. They be going to begin at Mrs. Estcourt's vust down to Greene Ferne. Her be sure to gie in to um, cos her's a 'ooman.
Rause: Odd drot um!
Tummas: I zay, Rause.
Rause: Eez, you.
Tummas: When be we a-goin to do it?
Rause: What dost mean?
Tummas: Up to church.
Rause: Thee ax Bob vust – he'll mash thee.
Tummas: I'll warm his jacket ef he puts a vinger on ee. Let's go up to paason.
Rause: Get on with thee.

Geoffrey heard a sound of struggling and two or three resonant kisses.

Tummas: Wooll ee come?
Rause: Go on whoam with thee.
Tummas: Danged ef I'll stand it! I wunt ax thee no more! Look ee here!
Rause: What's want?
Tummas: Woot, or wootn't?

Off went Rause at a run, and Tummas clattering after. Thought the listener, 'Was ever the important question put in straighter terms? Woot, or wootn't? Will you, or won't you?'

Tu-whit-tu-what! Steadily the scythe was swung, and the swathe fell in rows behind it.

CHAPTER III

THE NETHER MILLSTONE

THE HUGE water-wheel in the mill by Warren House went slowly round and round, grinding the corn. The ancient walls of the mill trembled under the ponderous motion, trembled but stood firm, as they had for centuries; so well did the monks see that their workmen mixed their mortar and dressed their stone in the days of the old world. A dull rumbling sound came from the chinks in the boarding that sheltered the wheel from the weather; a sound that could only be caused by an enormous mass in movement. Looking through into the semi-darkness, a heaving monster, black and direful, rolled continually past, threatening, as it seemed, to crush the life out of those who ventured within reach, as the stones within crushed form and shape out of the yellow wheat – the individual grain ground into the general powder. Yet the helpless corn by degrees wore away the solid adamant of its oppressor. Under the bowed apple-tree, clothed with moss, hard by, stood a millstone, grey and discoloured by the weather, thus rendered useless by the very corn it had so relentlessly annihilated.

Old Andrew Fisher sat at the mullioned western window of the house that stood higher up above the mill-pond, listening drowsily to the distant clack of the hopper. The mill, the manor-house, and many hundred fair acres of meadow and ploughed land and sheepwalk on the Down behind were his, and had been his forefathers' down from the days of the last Harry. More than one fair fortune had the mill ground out for them in the generations past; money – accumulated coin by coin, like the grains that together fill the bushel – accumulated by one and dissipated by the next. If report spoke truly, still another fortune had slowly piled itself up in Andrew's withered hand – weak in its grasp on his staff, but firm in its grasp on gold. Rich as he was known to be, he lived in the rude old way, spoke in the old rude tongue, and seemingly thought the old rude thought. His beehive-chair was drawn up close to the open window, so that the light air of the hot summer afternoon might wander in and refresh him.

High up in the cloudless azure, the swift, extending his wings like a black crescent, slid to and fro; the swallows, mere white specks in the dizzy blue, wheeled in ceaseless circles.

For ninety seasons, as man and boy – for three generations of thirty years each – had Andrew looked from that window. There he played in his childhood; there he rested from his labours in the time of manhood; there he sat in his old age. The deep gashes he had made with his first boy's clasp-knife still showed in the edge of the oaken window-seat. They were cut when the First Napoleon was winning his earlier victories. There on the seat he had drummed with his knuckles – one heavy knock with the left hand, then two with the right in quick succession, and an inch apart on the board to change the sound, imitating the noise of the mill. Thence he had noted the changing seasons and the cycle of the years.

Ninety times the snowdrop had hung her white flower under the sheltering wall. For ninety springs the corncrake's monotonous cry had resounded in the mowing-grass. The cuckoo came and went; the swallows sailed for the golden sands of the south; the leaves, brown and orange and crimson, dropped and died; the plover whistled over the uplands; the rain beat with pitiless fury against the pane, and swept before the howling blast along the fallow, ninety times.

Hard as his own nether millstone was the heart of Andrew Fisher. The green buds of spring, the flowers of summer, the fruits of autumn, the dead leaves of winter – all the beauty and the glory of nigh on a century touched him not. Unchanged at heart still, like the everlasting hills around him. But even they bear flowers – ling, loved by the bees, and thyme.

As flower and bird and leaf came and went, so the strong men with whom he had battled in his rude youth flitted away one by one to the meads of asphodel, but did not return in the spring. The carter whom he had partly blinded by a blow from his whip-handle, which injured an eyeball; the plough-boy he rode over and lamed; the fogger whose leg he broke with a kick in the old, old days, when brute force ruled irresponsibly on the wild hills – they slept peacefully under the greensward and the daisy. No more their weary bones would ache in the rain and snow; no more their teeth would grind the hard crust of toil. So, too, the old boon companions dropped away. Squire Thorpe – not the present, but the ancient one of evil days, wild and headstrong – was still enough at last in the vault under the chancel. He could swear and drink no more, nor fight a main of cocks every Sunday afternoon on his dining-room table. With his horny stiffened fingers Andrew could count up the houses in the hamlet at the Warren; there was not one that the hearse had not emptied. The hamlet of his youth had passed away. It is the aged that should see ghosts; there should be a spectre in every chair. The big black horse that carried him in the mad steeplechase at Millbourne – still talked of by the country-side – and in many a run with the Hunt in the vale, lay eight feet deep in the garden, and a damson-tree had grown over him.

Ninety times; and the scythe was busy in the grass, and the corn would soon turn colour yet once more.

Peggy was dead too – nut-brown Peggy, with her sloe-black eyes, *retroussée* nose, and mischievous mouth, who had reaped and gleaned and garnered her master's evil passion among convolvulus and poppy. Sweet Peggy, cast aside like the threshed-out straw, crushed, and broken, the light gone out in her eye, had forgotten her misery now the yew dropped its red berries on her resting-place. Fifty guineas, a heavy bribe in those days, the bailiff took to marry her. What a ghastly farce was celebrated that morn before God's holy altar! But the vicar's bulbous lips, that uttered those solemn words and jested, shall dip no more in the rosy wine they loved. He broke his neck when his horse fell at the double mound; but Andrew lives still. Peggy's boy, chained to the plough like a born serf, but full of his real father's fiery spirit, poached and stole, and worse, and at last laid his bones in the Australian gold rush.

Ninety times; and yet once more the wheat came on apace.

And Annica, Andrew's wife, cursed and beaten and bruised; and Andrew the younger, his lawful son, and Alice *his* wife, who were treated as dogs, and wore out their lives up at the farmstead farther in the hills: in Millbourne churchyard the moss has grown over their names graven on the sides of the great square tomb. May, their child, alone lived, a blithe and gentle creature, dreading her grim grandfather, only breathing freely when she could get away down to Greene Ferne, yet trying and schooling herself to love him; but hating Jane, the old snuff-taking house-keeper, as intensely as so affectionate a nature could hate anything.

Yet once more the swallows were wheeling in the summer air.

On the keystone of the porch was chiselled ANNO 15--; the other figures effaced, but cut some time in the century that saw the Armada. A vast, rambling, many-gabled, red-tiled building, with vines and cherries trained against the grey walls, and honeysuckle – creeping about the porch. The steep Downs rose behind, barely a gunshot distant; from Andrew's window there was an open view of the vale. The pool almost surrounded the garden – part moat, part fishpond, part mill-pool – and was crossed by a wooden bridge. There the moorhens swam and threw up their white-marked tails as they thrust their beaks under water; the timid dab-chick, which no familiarity with man can reassure, dived at the faintest footstep; the pike basked in the sunshine warming his cold blood, and the sturdy perch with tremulous tail faced the slow stream. By the stones of the sluice dark-green ferns flourished exceedingly. The sheep crept along the steep coombe-side cropping the short sweet grass; the shepherd sat on the edge and cut his own and his sweetheart's name in the turf. Time was when Andrew could run up the hill there light as a hare. Now his slow walk, hard bearing on blackthorn staff, in summer went no farther than the green before the porch, where the sundial stood with the motto on its brazen face, bidding men to number none but the happy hours, and to forget the dark and shadowy – a bitter mockery at fourscore and ten. In winter he crept twice or thrice a day across the courtyard to the barn, where, despite steam, he kept three old men at work on the threshing-floor – not for charity, but because he liked to listen to the knock-knock of the flails.

Ever round and round, without haste and without rest, went the massive wheel in the mill – ceaseless as the revolving firmament – to the clack of the noisy hopper and creak of the iron gudgeons, and the flousing splash of the mill-race. Hard as his own nether mill-stone was the heart of Andrew Fisher: does time soften the gnarled stem of the oak?

So he sat by the open window in his beehive chair that summer afternoon drowsily listening to the mill. In the window was the escutcheon of his family in coloured glass, and the name 'Fischere' in old-fashioned letters. Fishere of the Warren was fined one hundred pounds as a noted malignant in the days of fear and trembling that followed Worcester fight.

The shadow stole forward on the dial, and there came the dull hollow sound of horse's hoofs passing over the wooden bridge. Presently Jane the housekeeper, who, by virtue of her necessity to him in his infirmities, used no ceremony nor courtesy of speech, came in.

The Nether Millstone

'There be a paason wants to see thee,' said she.
No answer.
'Dost hear?'
A grunt.
'Wake up!' – shaking him.
He struck at her with his blackthorn that ever lay between his knees.
'Thee nistn't hoopy at I – I can hyar as well as thee,' he growled.
'A paason wants to see thee.'
'Ax un in.'
'Come in, you!' shouted the old hag, without going to the door. 'Shall I put thee jug away?' This to Andrew, and meaning the jug of weak gin-and-water which he kept constantly by him to sip.
'Let un bide.'
Felix St. Bees came into the room. He had ridden up to ask for the hand of May, his darling. It was not a reception to encourage a lover.
'Good afternoon, sir,' said Felix.
'Arternoon to ee.' To Jane, 'Who be it?'
'Dunno.'
'What's your wull wi' I?'
'I want a little private conversation with you, sir.'
'Get out, you!' to the ancient hag, who reluctantly walked from the room, but left the door ajar.
'Wull ee shut the door?'
Felix went and closed it. 'This is a fine old house,' he began, trying to get *en rapport* before opening his mission.
'Aw, eez.'
'And a beautiful view.'
'Mebbe.'
'You have had great experience of life, sir.'
'Likely zo.'
Andrew had had a good education in his youth, but lapsed two generations ago into broad provincialism. Now it had got about (as such things will) that Andrew was backing Val Browne's dark horse heavily, and May was anxious about her grandfather's intercourse with the trainer, who, except in his employer's eyes, was far from perfect. She

dreaded lest he should be cheated and lose the money – not so much for the sake of the amount, but because at his age and with his terrible temper it was impossible to say what effect it might have upon his health. So Felix, as a clergyman, wished to warn the aged man; but a little nervous (as might be pardoned under the circumstances) he did not, perhaps, go about it the right way.

'And you have seen, sir, how uncertain everything is – even the crops.'

'Wheat be vine this year.'

'Well, even your mill-wheel stops sometimes from accidents, I suppose.'

'Aw, a' reckon ull last my time. Wull re drenk?'

'No, thank you. The fact is I'm anxious to warn you about betting on Mr. Browne's horse. *He* is upright – but –'

'Hum!'

In the depths of his beehive-chair the glitter of the old man's grey eye was not observed by Felix.

'As you cannot get about and see for yourself, it seemed my duty to say something – for Miss Fisher's sake.'

'Aw!' ominously low and deep.

'I say for Miss Fisher's sake, because I am in hopes, with your permission, to visit her as her – her future husband, and as I am sure her happiness and – '

Crash!

The blackthorn whizzed by St. Bees' head and smashed the jug on the table.

'Jim! Bill! Jane! Jack!' shouted the old man, starting out of his chair, purple in the face. 'Drow this veller out! Douse un in th' hog-vault! Thee nimity-pimity odd-me-dod[19]! I warn thee'd like my money! Drot thee and thee wench!'

Poor Felix could do nothing but beat a retreat with half a dozen grinning chawbacons watching him over the bridge. On hearing their master's angry voice in the porch, they ran together from the rickyard in the rear. For some distance Felix could hear the old man howling and telling the men to 'zet th' dogs at un.' When he got fairly out of sight of the mill his indignation disappeared in his sense of the

---

[19] Little contemptible scarecrow.

ludicrous, and he burst into a hearty fit of laughter, and then sobered down again. 'For,' thought he, 'it is a wholesome doctrine – reverence for old age; and yet how little there is to revere! Ask this aged man's advice – you would suppose he would tell you of the vanity of the world, and instruct you to turn your mind to higher things. Not at all; he would say, "Get money; dismiss all generous feelings: get money." In the last decade of a century of life his avarice prompts him to risk heavy sums on this horse. But I must write and explain that *I* do not want his hoards.'

Calling at Greene Ferne on the way home to see May, he found everyone discussing the attitude of the labourers on the farm, who seemed inclined to neglect the haymaking, or even to leave it altogether. As the weather was fine and a large quantity of grass had been cut, it was a serious matter. Next morning Geoffrey Newton called on Felix – at his cottage in Kingsbury to tell him that the men had actually struck work, and that Mrs. Estcourt was anxious for his advice. For Felix, besides being a friend, was known to possess great influence among the working classes. Kingsbury town, though situate in the midst of a purely agricultural country, and not more than four or five miles distant from the oaks at Greene Ferne, was the seat of a certain manufacturing industry, which had immensely increased its population. It was the high wages paid in the factories and workshops there that made the agricultural labourers discontented; many walked miles daily to and fro to receive them. There was unfortunately a reverse side to the medal, for the overcrowded town had become notorious for disease, drunkenness, and misery. Now this was why Felix, with many opportunities of preferment, chose to remain a simple curate, in order that he might work among that grimy and boisterous people. Rude and brutal as they were, the little figure in black penetrated everywhere without risk, and was treated with the utmost respect.

It chanced to be his morning for visiting certain purlieus, so Geoffrey went with him. They were to go over to Greene Ferne in the evening. Down in the back streets they found that Melting-Pot, the pewter tankard, in full operation. Men and women were busy keeping it full, while their children, with naked feet, played in the gutter among the refuse of the dust heap, decayed cabbage, mangy curs, and filth. The ancient alchemists travailed to transmute the baser metals into gold; in these days whole townships are at work transmuting gold and silver into pewter. All the iron foundries, patent blasts, and Bessemer processes in the world cannot equal the melting power of the pewter tankard. When honest labour takes its well-earned draught it is one thing, or when friendship shares the glass; but the drinking for drinking's sake is another. Side by side with the Melting-Pot the furniture marts did a roaring business – marts where everything is sold, from a towel-horse to a piano or a cockatoo – sold beyond recall, all in the way of trade, and therefore quite legitimately. Is it not strange that while the law imposes fine and penalty on the pawnbroker, and strict supervision, the furniture mart, where the wretched drunkard's goods are sold for ever, seems to flourish without let or hindrance? 'Money advanced on goods for absolute sale,' is the notice prominently displayed, which to the poor artisan, being interpreted, reads, ' "Walk into my parlour," says the spider to the fly.' Geoffrey, who had been to Australia, found he was mistaken in thinking that he had seen the world. There were things here, close to the sweet fields of lovely England, not to be surpassed in the darkest corners of the earth. At the end of a new street hastily 'run up cheap' and 'scamped,' they found a large black pool, once a pond in the meadow, now a slough of all imaginable filth, at whose precipitous edge the roadway stopped abruptly, without rail, fence, or wall. Little children playing hare and hounds, heedless of their steps, fell in, and came out gasping, almost choked with foul mud. Drunken men staggered in occasionally, and came out stiff, ghastly, with slime in the greedy mouths that had gorged at the Melting-Pot. Yet this horrible slough was on the very verge of beauty; it was the edge and outpost of the town. Across this dark pit were green meadows, hawthorn hedges, and trees. The sweet breeze played against the dead red brick; odours of clover were blown against the windows; rooks came over now and then with their noisy caw-cawing. Shamefully 'scamped' was the row of six-roomed houses – doors that warped and would not shut, and so on. Upstairs, in one of these, they found a tall young fellow lying on his bed in the middle of the summer day. The sickly fetid smell of the close room told of long confinement. Poor fellow, he had been sore beset; unmarried, untended; no woman to potter about him, nursed anyhow, only the strength of his constitution carried him through; and now he lay there, weak and helpless, in spirit all but dead, as strong men are after tedious illness. A mass of iron had fallen on his leg in one of the factories some time before, as it was supposed through the carelessness of a fellow-workman not recovered from his weekly orgie of drink. The sturdy limb, though it had long ago united, was still feeble in the extreme. His dull eye lit up when he saw them.

'You bean't from Millbourne, be you?' he said.

'We know many there,' said Felix.

'I thaut perhaps uncle Jabez had found me out and sent ee. Do you knaw uncle Jabez, as works at Greene Ferne?'

'I recollect the shepherd,' said Geoffrey.

'I wur under shepherd thur till I took to factory work. Look at them lambs thur!'

They looked out of the window. Beneath, the green fields came right up to the dead brick wall. Away, some fifty yards distant, stood an enormous pollard oak, its vast gnarled root coiled round just above the earth, forming a broad ledge about the trunk. Half a dozen lambs were chasing each other, frisking round and round the rim, glad in the summer sunshine.

'Look at um,' said the whilom shepherd, 'an' I be choked for aair.'

'Why not open the window?'

'He wunt open.'

They examined it; the sashes were shams, *not made to open*. Neither was there a fireplace; the man was poisoned with the exhalations from his own weak frame.

'This is dreadful,' said Geoffrey. 'Is there no law – '

'Law enough,' said Felix, bitterly; 'but who troubles to enforce it for the sake of – a navvy? Why are crowded places sinks of misery and crime? For want of a Master, like the colonel of a regiment. It makes me sigh for a despot.'

'I'd a' smashed un fast enough,' said the shepherd, 'if I'd a-dared; but thaay ud 'a turned me out into the street, an' I couldn't abear the workuss. Is ould Fisher dead yet, zur?'

St. Bees was busy with his penknife cutting away the putty, and did not for the moment answer. The pane came out speedily, and the breeze came in with a rush, and with it a bee that buzzed round and went forth again, and a scent of new-made hay, and the 'Baa – maa' of the lambs, and behind it all the low roar of the railway and the factories.

'What did you say about Fisher?' asked Felix, turning.

'Be a' dead yet, th' cussed old varmint?'

'Hush, hush! whom do you mean?'

'I means ould Fisher of Warren Mill. He be my grandfeyther. Mebbe you minds Peggy Moulding, what married th' bailie? Hur wur my granny. My feyther died in Australia. Th' cussed ould varmint – a let us all starve; he got sacks a' gold. I wants to hear as th' devil have got un.'

'You must not bear malice,' said Felix; but being a man as well as a clergyman, he halted there. The contrast was too great. He thought of the brutal miser on the hills.

'I wants to get back to Greene Ferne,' said the invalid. 'Do you knaw Mrs. Estcourt? Hur be a nice ooman; a' wunder ef hur ud have me agen. Wull ee ax hur?'

'I'll ask her,' said Geoffrey. 'I'm sure she will, though the men are on strike there now.'

'Be um? Lord, what vools! I wants to get back to shepherding. Ax uncle Jabez ef I med come to his place and bide wi' he a bit. I thenks I should get better among the trees. I could a'most drag a rake, bless ee, now ef I had some vittels.'

'You shall have food,' said Felix, 'and we will get you back to the hamlet.' This poor fellow, rude as he was – so pathetically ignorant as to suppose, as ignorant people do, that strangers understood his private affairs – was in a sense distantly related to his darling May, and thus had a more than common claim upon him.

In the afternoon they went over to Greene Ferne, and Mrs. Estcourt at once sent a trap for the injured man. His uncle Jabez, the shepherd, was greatly concerned, and ready to receive him. Yet, with the curious apathy of the poor, he had made no inquiries about him previously.

CHAPTER IV

THE WOODEN BOTTLE

'G EE, DIAMOND! Now, Captain!' cried Margaret, imitating the gruff voice of the carter. Crack! The long-knotted lash of the waggon-whip, bound about the handle with brazen rings, whistled in the air and curled up with a vicious snap. She was in one of her wild impulsive moods. Away trotted the two huge carthorses, the harness merrily jingling and the waggon jolting. Jabez the shepherd could hardly keep pace with it, running beside the leader, Diamond. Margaret and May were riding. Crack! Crack!

'Aw, doan't ee now – doan't ee, miss!' panted the shepherd. 'Us ull go right drough th' winder! Whoa!'

For they were steering straight for the great window at Greene Ferne that opened on the lawn. It was wide open that beautiful midsummer morning.

'What are those children doing?' said Mrs. Estcourt, in some alarm. 'Why, they have harnessed the horses!'

Valentine, Geoffrey, and Felix, who were there, crowded to the window.

'Whoa, Diamond! Captain, whoa!' cried Margaret, bringing up her convoy on the lawn in fine style. 'Now, mamma clear, jump up! We're all going haymaking, as the men won't.'

'She has solved the problem,' said Valentine. 'Here's one volunteer!' And he sprang up.

That very morning they had been holding a council to see if anything could be suggested to put an end to the strike. It had now lasted nearly a fortnight. Felix in vain argued with the men; they listened respectfully, and even admitted that he was right; but all they would say was that 'they meaned to have th' crownd.'

Slow to take action, there is no one so stubborn, when once he has resolved, as the agricultural labourer. They had timed the strike with some cunning. They had let the mowers cut some sixty acres of grass, and then suddenly stopped work. They knew very well that if cut grass is allowed to remain exposed to the sun longer than just sufficient to make it into hay, it dries up so much as to be of little value. Now the burning brilliant summer sunshine had been pouring down upon the withered grass for days and days, expelling every particle of the succulent sap, and turning it to a brittle straw. The shepherd, Jabez, remained at his work, and he and Augustus Basset, the 'bailie,' did a little, throwing up a mead or two into 'wakes' for carting; but their exertions were of small avail. While they talked and deliberated, Margaret, beckoning May, slipped out and went down to the stables. Diamond and Captain were led out into the sunshine, and stood like statuary, waiting to be bidden. For the beauty of simple strength nothing equals a fine carthorse: the vast frame, the ponderous limb, the massive neck, speak of power in repose. Their large dark lustrous eyes followed the girls with calm astonishment; but, docile and gentle, they gave implicit obedience to orders. The heavy harness, brass-mounted, was as much as ever the two girls could manage to lift; and when it came to hoisting up the shafts of the waggon they were at a loss. But Jabez, hearing a noise at the stables, came up; and after him slouched Augustus, muttering to himself, as usual. So just when the council indoors was beginning to wonder what had become of Margaret and May, crack, crack, and the jingling of harness put an end to their deliberations.

Geoffrey quickly followed Valentine; Felix, more thoughtful, brought a chair for Mrs. Estcourt, who, half laughing, half protesting, against Margaret's wilful fancy, got up. Augustus sat on the shafts, Jabez stood by the leader, and, seeing them all in, started for the field.

'If you were to bring out a thirty-six-gallon cask,' said Augustus, whose red nose peered over the front part of the waggon, 'and set it up on a haycock, I'll warn them chaps would come back fast enough.' This was one word for the haymakers and two for himself.

'I'm sure I don't grudge them some ale,' said Mrs. Estcourt. 'But they are really very unreasonable. One of the servants took a mower a quart of beer. He said he did not like it, and didn't want so much, and poured it out on the grass. Next day only a pint was sent to him: "Why y'ent you brought me a quart?" said he. "Because you flung it away," was the reply. "Aw, that don't matter. You bring I a quart. I'll have my mishure" [measure]; nor should I mind paying the extra five shillings; but you see, Felix, if I pay it, all the farmers round – for they have only struck work on my place, thinking, no doubt, that, being a woman, I must give way – will be obliged to do so, and some of them are not able. Many have called and begged me not; and Mr. Thorpe says the same. Yet I don't like it. We have always been on good terms with the men.'

'O yes, you pets 'em up,' said Augustus, 'just like so many children; and, of course, they ain't going to work for you.'

'The struggle of capital and labour,' began Felix learnedly, when a sudden jolt of the springless waggon threw him off his balance, and he had to cling to the sides.

'O, mind the gatepost!' cried Mrs. Estcourt, in some alarm.

While they were near the house Jabez went slow; but the moment he reached the open field away he started, and what with the jingling of the harness, the creaking of the wheels, and the necessity for holding on tight, conversation became impossible. The waggon rose up and sloped down over the furrows of the meadow as a boat pitches in a sea.

'Woaght! whoa!' shouted Jabez, drawing up among the hay. 'This be it; the prongs be in the ditch.'

When they had descended, he went to the hawthorn bush, pulled out some prongs, and then scrambled up into the waggon himself. 'Now then, you lards and gennelmen, one on ee get each side, and pitch up thaay wakes [ridges of hay put ready for the purpose of loading], and mind as you doan't stick your farks into I. The wimmen – I means the ladies – wull rake behind, and paason can help um – th' rakes be hung on th' hedge. Now, bailie, look arter them 'osses.'

Though hay looks light and easy to lift, yet when the fork has gathered a goodly bundle, to hoist it high overhead, and continue the operation, is really heavy labour. Valentine was physically a smaller made man than Geoffrey, whose broad shoulders had also been developed both by athletic exercise at home and by work in Australia – work done from choice, not necessity. But though smaller, Valentine was extremely tough, wiry, and nimble, as is often the case with gentlemen who 'fancy' horses. Quick in his movements, he caught the knack of 'pitching' almost immediately. He hastily flung up his 'wake' as far as the horse in the shafts, and then walked to the rear of the waggon where Margaret was raking, leaving Geoffrey still engaged.

Margaret and May were looking at a nest of harvest-trows, as the tiny mice are called that breed in the grass. Valentine began to talk about his horses, knowing Margaret was fond of animals, and said that a 'string' of his would pass Greene Ferne in the evening *en route* to his stables. Now Geoffrey, glancing back, saw the group apparently in earnest conversation from which he was excluded; and noting Margaret's attention to Valentine, grew jealous and angry. Just as he finished 'pitching,' and was about to join them –

'Tchek!' from Augustus, and on the horses moved, and he had to recommence work. Valentine ran with his prong, and again, by dint of great exertions, finished his side first, and returned to Margaret.

'Tchek! woaght!'

The third time Valentine essayed the same task, delighted to leave Geoffrey in the cold, and to exhibit his superior prowess. But Geoffrey by now had learned how to handle his fork. His muscles were strung, his blood was up, he warmed to his work and pitched vast bundles that all but buried and half choked Jabez, who was loading on the waggon.

'The dust be all down my droat! Aw, doan't ee, measter!' he cried, in smothered tones.

'Tchek!' and this time Valentine was far behind, and Geoffrey had gone back to talk to Margaret. At the next move Geoffrey not only cleared his side up to the horse in the shafts, but by using his great strength to the utmost, went ahead up the wake eight or ten yards, and thus secured himself twice as long with her, while Valentine had to remain 'pitching.' To Jabez the shepherd, on the waggon, it was fine sport to watch the rivalry of the 'gennelmen.' A labouring man thoroughly enjoys seeing the perspiration pouring from the faces of the well-to-do. He bustled about as fast as he could, and kept the horses moving. By superior muscular force Geoffrey remained ahead. To Valentine it was gall and wormwood.

'We be getting on famous, zur,' said Jabez. 'Tchek!'

Mrs. Estcourt had meantime left the field, after beckoning to Augustus, who followed her. While she was present there was some check on their rivalry; but no sooner did they perceive that she was gone than it rose to a still greater height. Valentine, pulling himself together, and taking advantage of a thinner wake than usual, ran ahead, and went back to the rear. Seeing this, Geoffrey hurled the hay up with such force and vigour that he literally covered the shepherd, who could barely struggle out of it.

'Lord, I be as dry as a gicks!' said Jabez, when he did get free, and meaning by his simile the stem of a dead hedge-plant.

'And here's bailie wi' th' bottle. Bide a bit, my lards.'

By this time 'my lards' thoroughly understood why haymakers like their ale, and plenty of it. Working under the hot sun, with the dust or dry pollen flying from the hay, causes intense thirst. So the waggon stood still, and Valentine, hot and angry, took the bottle – being the nearest – from Augustus, and essayed to drink. This 'bottle' was a miniature cask of oaken staves, with iron hoops, and a leathern strap to carry it by. It held about a gallon. To drink, the method is to put the lips to the bung-hole, situate at the largest part of the circumference, toss the barrel up, and hold the head back. Valentine could not get more than the merest sip, though the bottle was quite full. This, scientifically speaking, was caused by the pressure of the atmosphere. There is the same difficulty in drinking from a flask.

'Let th' aair in – let th' aair in!' said the shepherd, himself an adept. 'Open th' carner of yer mouth.'

But attempting to do that Val let too much 'aair' in, and spilt the ale, to his intense disgust.

'Put th' cark in, zur, and chuck un up to I.' Jabez caught the 'bottle' as tenderly as a mother would her infant, and quitted not his hold till half the contents had disappeared, nor would he have left it then, had not Augustus grumbled and claimed his turn. Mrs. Estcourt now returned, attended by a servant carrying a basket of refreshments for which she had gone, not forgetting the more civilised bottles issued by the divine Bass. Throwing down forks and rakes, they assembled in the shade of the tall hawthorn hedge and sat down on the hay. When the delicate flavour of his cigar floated away on the soft summer air, even Valentine's acerbity of temper relaxed. Opposite, at some distance, stood the waggon now fully loaded; Diamond and Captain eating the hay put for them, and the shepherd lying at full length on the grass. Augustus, the 'bottle' by his side, and his hand laid lovingly on it, fell asleep in the shade of the waggon.

The wild-roses on the briars that stretched out from the hedge towards the meadow opened their petals full to the warmth. The breeze rustled the leaves of the elm overhead. Rich flute-like notes of music came from the copse hard by – it was the blackbird.

'Ah, this is merry England,' said Felix, who loved his cigar, watching the tiny cloud float away from its tip. 'The blackbird sings in the scorching sun at noonday, when the other songbirds are silent. You did not know Geof was a writer, did you?' He drew forth a piece of paper, when Newton began to protest, and would have taken it from him by main force, had not the ladies insisted on hearing the contents. So Felix read the verses.

NOONTIDE IN THE MEADOW

> Idly silent were the finches –
> Finches fickle, fleeting, blithe;
> And the mower, man of inches,
> Ceased to swing the sturdy scythe.
>
> All the leafy oaks were slumb'rous;
> Slumb'rous e'en the honey-bee;
> And his larger brother, cumbrous,
> Humming home with golden knee.
>
> But the blackbird, king of hedgerows –
> Hedgerows to my memory dear –
> By the brook, where rush and sedge grows,
> Sang his liquid love-notes clear.

Margaret, toying with a June rose – the white petal delicately tinted with pink between her soft rosy fingers – dreamily repeated half to herself,

> 'All the leafy oaks were slumb'rous.'

Valentine glanced at her swiftly, and inwardly resolved to remove the impression on her mind. He took out his pocket-book.

'My verses,' said he, 'are only copied, but they seemed to me a gem in their way. It is a piece of Bacchic meditation from the Vaux de Vire, exquisitely translated by some clever author whose name I have forgotten. You are gazing at our friend Augustus' bibulous nose,' he nodded towards the recumbent figure with the hand on the bottle, 'and see it through your own glass:

> 'Fair nose! whose beauties many pipes have cost

Of white and rosy wine;
Whose colours are so gorgeously embossed
In red and purple fine;
Great nose, who views thee, gazing through great glass,
Thee still more lovely thinks.
Thou dost the nose of creature far surpass
Who only water drinks.'

It was so appropriate to poor Augustus that they could not choose but smile. Valentine begged Margaret to sing: they all joined in the request, and she sang with a faint blush, looking down – for she knew, though the rest did not, that it was Geoffrey's favourite – the beautiful old ballad of the 'Bailiff's Daughter of Islington.' With the wild-rose in her hand, the delicate bloom on her cheek, the green hedge behind, the green elm above, and the sweet scent of the hay, she looked the ballad as well as sang it.

'Ah,' said Felix, 'no sign of study in those old ballads, no premeditation, no word-twisting and jerking; rugged metre so involved that none can understand it without pondering an hour or two. This is the way we criticise poetry now-a-days, in our mechanical age – just listen: somebody has been measuring Tennyson with a foot-rule. I read from a professor's analysis – "The line is varied by dactylic or iambic substitution, as well as by truncation and anacrusis;" "the line is varied by anapaestic and trochaic (rarely dactylic) substitutions, and by initial truncation." As Faust says, not all these word-twisters have ever made a Maker yet.'

Crash! – splintering of wood and breaking of boughs.

'Here gwoes! Come on, you! Hoorah! Us ull put it up, missus; doan't ee be afeared! you bin a good missus to we. So into't, you vellers!'

Eight or ten men came crashing through a gap in the hedge, and seizing the prongs and rakes that were lying about with no more explanation than these brief ejaculations, dashed out to work. Heartily tired of rambling idly about, hands in pockets, seeing no prospect of the men on the other farms joining them, they had been hanging round the place in a sheepish way, till, finally observing the ladies working, the sense of shame got the better, and they made a rush for the hay, and gave up the strike. For there is sterling worth and some rude chivalry in these men, though simple enough, and easily led astray; the more the pity that no one has yet taken the lead among them with a view to their own real and solid advancement.

'I will go home and send them some refreshment,' said Mrs. Estcourt. All the party rose and accompanied her. In the next field they passed the mowers preparing to begin mowing again. Geoffrey and Valentine both tried to mow, but utterly failed; the point of the scythe persistently stuck into the ground.

'A' be a' akkerd tool for a body as bean't used to un,' said the eldest of the men, taking out his stone rubber from the sling at his back, preparatory to giving the scythe a touch up after such rough handling; 'and um bean't what um used to be when I wur a bwoy.'

'How do you mean?' said Felix.

'Aw,' said the mower, tilting his hat back, 'th' blades be as good as ever um wur – thaay folk at Mells be th' vellers to make scythes. Thur bean't none as good as thairn. But it be th' handle, look ee, as I means. I minds when thaay wur made of dree sarts of wood, a main bit more crooked than this yer stick, and sart o' carved a bit; doant ee see? It took a chap a week zumtimes to find a bit a' wood as ud do. But, bless ee, a'moast anything does now.'

Swish went the keen blade through the tall grass. They watched him a few minutes.

'Thur be some blight about,' said the man; 'scythe do scum up terrable,' and he showed them the blade all covered with a greenish-white froth, supposed to be caused by insects. 'Thur be blight up thur, look.'

He pointed to a dark heavy cloud that seemed to float at a great height in the east.

'It will thunder,' said May.

'Aw, no it wunt, miss,' said the mower. 'A' reckon as it'll be nation hot; thuck cloud be nothing but blight. Spile the fruit, bless ee.'

'So even the scythe handles used to be artistic,' said Felix, as they walked away. 'There used to be art and taste and workmanship even in so common a thing. It was made of three distinct pieces of wood, carefully finished off; men took days to find a piece. Now it is nothing but a stick smoothed by machinery. I *hate* machinery. I like to see the artist in his work; to see the mark of the knife where the chip has been taken out. But the spirit of art flies when things are sent forth by machinery – hundreds exactly alike.'

To May it was a great pleasure to hear him dilate in this way. Near the house they met Augustus, radiant with smiles, and perfectly loaded with the wooden bottles for the men.

'I knows I'm a fool,' said he; 'at least I ought to, since I'm told so forty times a day. But a fool must be sometimes right. Tend upon it, there's nothing like ale!'

At Greene Ferne, May found a letter for her which spoilt the day. It was from her grandfather, Andrew Fisher, of the Warren, written in great anger, and commanding her immediate return home, and to mind and bring that rug with her that had been at Greene Ferne ever since Christmas. The old grasping miser, in his rage, remembered such a trifle as a travelling-rug. Fisher had sent a verbal message for his granddaughter before, which she had ventured to put off; now he wrote in a furious temper, and added at the foot that if that parson ever came anigh the Warren again he'd have him ducked in the mill-pool. So bitter had the mere thought made him that Felix wanted his money. There was nothing for it but for May to return, and she asked for her horse to be saddled. Felix could hardly suppress his annoyance. May was much downcast, but Margaret cheered her.

'I will go with you,' she said. 'He was always nice to me. He is a regular old flatterer' – (she peeped in the glass) – 'only think, flattering at ninety! But a man must flatter, if he's a hundred! I shall get over him! I'll ride my chestnut, and I can stay with you, dear, can't I? and come back next evening.'

So they left together. Geoffrey, in shaking hands with Margaret, tried to whisper, 'May I come and meet you tomorrow evening?' but could not well manage, it, Valentine being near.

'Be sure and return by the road, dear,' said Mrs. Estcourt – 'the Downs are very lonely if you come by yourself, and you may lose your way.'

'Oh, no,' laughed Margaret. 'I love the hills, and I know them all. I must come over the turf, mamma dear.'

Now, Geoffrey heard this, and mentally noted it. He had his horse at Thorpe Hall, and he determined to ride and meet Margaret on the morrow.

CHAPTER V

EVENING

Aw, AIM FOR TH' TUMP, measter; aim for th' Tump,' said the carter, slanting his whip to indicate the direction. 'When you gets thur, look ee, go for th' Cas'l; and when you gets thur, go athwert the Vuzz toward th' Virs; and when you gets drough thaay, thur be Akkern Chace, and a lane as goes down to Warren. Tchek! Woaght!'

At the foot of the Downs, along whose base the highway-road wound, Geoffrey had paused to take counsel of a carter, who had just descended with a load of flints, before venturing across the all-but-trackless hills. The man very civilly stopped his waggon and named the various landmarks by which he would have guided his own course to Andrew Fisher's. Geoffrey had started early in the evening, intending to go all the way to Warren House, for he carried with him the rug (strapped to the saddle) which Margaret and May had forgotten, and for which the rude old man had written. This rug, which Mrs. Estcourt gave him, was in fact his passport, for he scarcely knew how Margaret would take his coming to fetch her in that rather abrupt way. Guessing what the man meant more by the slant of his whip than his words, he turned off the road on to the sward, and ascended the hill.

A long narrow shadow of man and horse, disproportionately stretched out, raced before him along the slope. The hoofs of the grey hardly cut the firm turf, dry with summer heat; the vivid green of spring had already gone, and a faint brown was just visible somewhere in the grass. Dark boulder stones – sarsens – bald and smooth, thrust their shoulders out of the sward here and there; hollowed out into curious cuplike cavities, in which, after a shower, the collected raindrops remained imprisoned in tiny bowls hard as the fabled adamant of mediæval story. Round white bosses – white as milk, and globular like cannon-shot – dotted the turf, fungi not yet ripened into the dust of the puff-ball. Now and again the iron shoes dashed an edible mushroom to pieces, turning the pink gills upwards to shrivel and blacken in the morrow's sun. The bees rose with a shrill buzz from the white clover, which is the shepherd's sign of midsummer. Swiftly the grey sped along the slopes, the shadow racing before grew longer and fainter as the beams of the sun came nearly horizontally. Already the ridges cast a shadow into the hollows – into the narrow coombes, where great flints and chalk fragments had rolled down and strewed the ground as with the wreck of a titanic skirmish. Thickets of green furze tipped with yellow bloom, and beneath, peeping out, the pale purple heath-flower. On the stunted hawthorn-bushes standing alone, stern sentinels in summer's heat and winter's storm, green peggles hardening, which autumn would redden and ripen for the thrush. Odorous thyme and yellow-bird's-foot lotus embroidering the grassy carpet; wide breadths of tussocky grass, tall and tough, which the sheep had left untouched, and where the hare crouched in her form, hearkening to the thud of the hoofs.

On past the steep wall of an ancient chalk-quarry, spotted with red streaks and stains as of rusty iron, where the plough-boys search for pyrites, and call them thunderbolts and 'gold,' for when broken the radial metallic fibres glisten yellow. Past a field of oats, rising hardly a foot high in the barren soil – in the corner an upturned plough with rusty share and wooden handles painted red. Down below in the plains between the hills squares of drooping barley and bold upstanding wheat, whose tender green the sun had invaded with advancing hues of gold. Over all the brooding silence of the summer eve, one brown lark alone singing in the air above the plain, far away from the distant ridge the faint tinkle of a sheepbell. Now the sun was down the lower eastern atmosphere thickened with a dull red; the shepherds discerned the face of the sky, and said to-morrow would be fine.

Up the steep side of the 'Tump' at last, slackening speed perforce, and checking the grey on the summit. It was a great round hill, detached, and somewhat like a huge bowl inverted, with a small circular level space, on what at a distance seemed an almost pointed apex, a space bare of aught but close-cropped herbage. Westwards was the dim vale, a faint mist blotting out steeple and tower – a mist blending with the sky at the horizon, and there all aglow. Eastwards, ridge upon ridge, hill after hill, with spurs running out into the narrow plains between, and deep coombes. He gazed earnestly over these, looking for signs and landmarks, but found none. The rough trail was lost – the hoof-marks cut in the winter when the earth was soft were filled up by the swelling turf, and covered over with thyme. Those who laboured by day in the plains, weeding the fields, were gone down to their homes in the hamlets hidden in the valleys. At a venture he struck direct for the east, anxious to lose no time; for he began to fear he should miss Margaret, and soon afterwards luckily crossed the path of a shepherd-lad, whistling as he and his shaggy dog wended for 'whoam.'

'Which is the way to Mr. Fisher's?' asked Geoffrey.

'Thaay be goin' into th' Mash to-morrow,' answered the boy, whose thoughts were differently engaged.

'Tell me the way to Mr. Fisher's – the Warren.'

'We be got shart o' keep; wants zum rain, doan't ee zee?'

'Can't you answer a question?'

'Thur's a main sight o' tackle in the Mash vor um.'

He was so used to being stopped and asked about his sheep that he took it for granted Geoffrey was putting the same accustomed interrogatories. Every farmer cross-examines his neighbour's shepherd when he meets him. The 'Mash' was doubtless a meadow reclaimed from a marsh.

'Land be terrable dry, zur.'

'Will you listen to me?' angrily. 'Where's the Warren?'

'Aw, mebbe you means ould Fisher's?'

'I mean Mr. Fisher's.'

'A' be auver thur,' pointing north-east.

'How far?'

'Aw, it be a akkerd road,' doubtfully, as he looked Geoffrey up and down, and it dawned on him slowly that it was a stranger.

'I'll give you a quart if you will show me.'

'Wull ee? Come on.' The beer went at once right to the nervous centre and awoke all his faculties. He led Geoffrey across the plain and up a swelling shoulder of down, on whose ridge was a broad deep fosse and green rampart.

'This be th' Cas'l,' said the guide, meaning entrenchments – earthworks are called 'castles.' In one spot the fosse was partly filled up, and an opening cut in the rampart, by which he rode through and found the 'castle,' a vast earthwork of unknown antiquity.

'Mind thaay vlint-pits,' said the boy.

The flint-diggers had been at work here long ago – deep gullies and holes encumbered the way, half-hidden with thistles and furze. The place was honeycombed; it reminded Geoffrey of the Australian gold-diggings. He threaded his way slowly between these, and presently emerged on the slope beyond the 'castle.'

'Now which way is it?' he asked, glancing doubtfully at the hills still rolling away in unbroken succession.

'Yellucks,' said the boy, meaning 'Look here,' and he pointed at a dark object on a distant ridge, which Geoffrey made out to be a copse. 'Thur's Moonlight Virs.'

'Well, and when I get to Moonlight Firs, which way then?'

'Thee foller th' ruts – thaay'll take ee to Akkern Chace.'

'The ruts?'

'Eez, th' waggon ruts; thaay goes drough Akkern Chace down to Warren. Be you afeared?' seeing Geoffrey hesi-

Evening

tated. 'Thaay'll lead ee drough th' wood; it be main dark under th' pollard oaks:

> Akkern Chace
> Be a unkid place,
> When th' moon do show hur face.

Wur be my quart?'

Geoffrey gave him sixpence; he touched his forelock, called his dog, and whistled down the hill. Geoffrey pushed on as rapidly as his horse, now a little weary, would go for the firs. In half an hour he reached it, and found a waggon track which, as the boy had said, after a while led him into a wood – scattered pollard oaks, hawthorn bushes, and fir plantations. Now two fresh difficulties arose: the grey first limped and then went lame; and the question began to arise, Would Margaret after all come this way? In the gathering twilight, might she not take the circuitous, but safer, highway? She might even have already passed. By this time he was well into the wood – it consisted of firs there. The grey went so lame he resolved to go no farther, but to wait. He dismounted, threw himself at length upon the grass beside the green track, and the grey immediately applied himself to grazing with steady contentment.

The tall green trees shut out all but a narrow lane of sky, azure, but darkening; not the faintest breath of moving air relieved the sultry brooding heat of the summer twilight. From the firs came a fragrance, filling the atmosphere with a sweet resinous odour. The sap exuding through the bark formed in white viscous drops upon the trunks. Indolently reclining, half drowsy in the heat, he could see deep into the wood, along on the level ground between the stems, for the fallen 'needles' checked vegetation. A squirrel gambolled hither and thither in this hollow space; with darting rapid movements it came towards him, and then suddenly shot up a fir and was instantly out of sight among the thick foliage. In the stillness he could hear the tearing of the fibres of grass as the grey fed near. A hare came stealing up the track, with the peculiar shuffling, cunning gait they have when rambling as they deem unwatched. Limping slowly, 'Wat' stayed to choose tit-bits among the grass – so near that when an insect tickled him and he shook his head Geoffrey heard the tips of his ears flap together. Daintily he pushed his nose among the tussocks, then craned his neck and looked into the thickets. Where the track turned at the bend the shadows crept out, toning down the twilight with mystic uncertainty.

Suddenly the hare rose, elevated his ears – Geoffrey could see the nostrils working – and then, with one thrust as it were of his lean flanks, flung himself into the wood. The grey ceased feeding, raised his head, and listened. In a few moments came the slow thud of hoofs walking. From behind the bushes Geoffrey watched the bend of the track. Then the sweet voice he knew so well floated towards him. Margaret was singing, little thinking any one was near:

>'And as she went along the high-road,
>   The weather being hot and dry,
>   She sat her down upon a green bank,
>   And her true love came riding by.'

Her chestnut whinnied, seeing the other horse on turning the corner.

'Margaret!'

'Sir!' blushing, and resentful that he should have surprised her. She had been thinking of him. She felt as though he had caught her and discovered her secret. She instantly took refuge in hauteur.

'I came to meet you.'

'Thank you,' extremely coldly; she was passing on.

'You do not mind?' he took hold of her bridle.

'Mr. Newton!' angrily. Her countenance became suffused with a burning red. He felt he had blundered.

'At least you will let me ride back with you,' he said humbly, dropping the bridle.

She immediately struck the chestnut – the mare sprang forward and cantered down the lane. Quite beside himself, half with annoyance with her, half with himself, he ran to the grey, mounted, and tried to follow. But the horse was lame. He did his best, limped, stumbled, recovered himself, and shambled after painfully. When Geoffrey reached the edge of the wood, Margaret, a long distance ahead, was rid-

Evening

ing out upon the Downs – horse and horsewoman a dark figure, indistinct in the gloaming. Fearful of losing her, he called on the grey; but she glided away from him swiftly over the darkening plain and up the opposite hill. For a moment he saw her clear against the sky-line, then she was over the ridge and gone.

He thrashed the grey, and forced him rather than rode him up the hill, but there the long-suffering animal stayed his wretched shamble and walked. Wild with anger, Geoffrey dismounted, ran to the edge of the hill, and looked for Margaret.

Deep in the wide hollow lay a white mist, covering all things with its cloak. Beyond was a black mass, with undulating ridge against the sky. 'The chestnut *must* walk up that,' he thought; and, without a moment's pause, dropped his whip, and raced down the slope headlong. What he should say or do if he overtook her he did not stay to think; but overtake her he would. His long stride carried him quickly to the bottom. He imagined he should find a thick fog there as it had looked from above; but now that he was in it there was nothing more than an impalpable mist, through which he could see for some distance. But upwards the mist thickened, and the hill above was hidden now.

He listened – not a sound; then rushed across the level, and threw himself against the next ascent. Panting, he reached the summit; it was but a narrow ridge, and over it another coombe. Instead of a sea of mist here, one long streak, like a cloud, hung midway. No horse visible. Again he dashed forward, and passed through the stratum of mist-cloud as he went down, and the second time as he clomb the opposite rise – more slowly, for these Downs pull hard against the strongest chest. Then there was a gradually rising plateau – dusky, dotted with ghostly hawthorn bushes, but nothing moving that his straining eyes could discern.

But as he stood, and his labouring heart beat loudly, there came the faint sound of iron-shod hoofs that clicked upon stray flints, far away to the right. Like an arrow he rushed there – unthinking, and therefore baffled. For in-

Greene Ferne Farm

stead of crossing the steep ridges, she had ridden round on the slope; and he, running on the chord of the arc, had not only caught her up, but got some distance in front. If he had remained where he was, she would have passed close by him. But running thus to the right in his wild haste, he lost great part of his advantage. Suddenly he stopped short, and saw in the dim light a shadowy figure stretching swiftly into the mist.

'Margaret!' he called, involuntarily. The earth-cloud of mist closed round her, and the shadowy figure faded away. On he went again, stumbling in the ruts left by wheels in winter, nearly thrown by the tough heath, and the crooked furze stems holding his foot, and fast losing his wind. He struggled up the slope, and finally, perforce, came to a striding walk. Suddenly he stopped – a low neigh floated in the stillness up from a vale on his left. Her path turned there, then; he would cut across the angle. But, taught by experience, he paused at the edge of the descent, and listened before going down. In a minute or two another faint clicking of flints sounded behind him. 'By Jove, I begin to think – aha!' The flints clicked in the stillness away on his right. Then after a brief while a dark indistinct object crossed in front of him. 'All round me,' said Geoffrey, aloud. 'I understand.' He bounded forward, refreshed by his short pause. In three minutes the dark object resolved itself into the chestnut, standing still now on the verge of a gloomy hollow.

Then, close upon his quarry, the hunter slackened speed. It was his turn now; he strolled slowly, halted, even turned his back upon her, and looked up at the sky. The stars were shining; till that moment he had not realised that it was night. By-and-by he went nearer.

'Geoffrey!' she called, faintly. No reply.

'Geoffrey!' – louder – 'is that you?'

'Yes, dear.' The first time he had used the word to her.

'Do come to me!' in a tone of distress. He ran eagerly to her side.

'It is dark,' she said, in a low voice, 'and – and I have lost the way.'

'I thought you had; you rode all round me.'

Evening

'Did I? O, then I am lost, indeed; that is what people always do when they are lost on the hills – they go round and round in a circle. Where is your horse?'

'I left him lame, a long way behind.'

'How unfortunate! And "Kitty"' – stroking the mare's neck- 'is weary too. But perhaps you know the way – try and look.'

He did look round to please her, but with little hope. It was not indeed dark – unless there are clouds, the nights of summer are not dark – but the dimness that results from uncertain definition was equally bewildering. The vales were full of white mist; the plains visible near at hand grew vague as the eye tried to trace a way across. The hills, just where the ridges rose high, could be seen against the sky, but the ranges mingled and the dark slopes faded far away into the mist. Each looked alike – there was no commanding feature to fix the vision; hills after hills, grey shadowy plains, dusky coombes and valleys, dimly seen at hand and shapeless in the distance. Then he stooped and searched in vain for continuous ruts or hoof marks or any sign of track. She watched him earnestly.

'It is difficult to make out,' he said. 'You know I am a stranger to these Downs.'

'Yes, yes; what shall we do? I shall not reach Greene Ferne to-night.'

'I will try very hard,' he said, venturing to take her hand. But in his heart he was doubtful.

CHAPTER VI

NIGHT

MARGARET did not remove her hand from Geoffrey's grasp, partly because her mind was occupied with the difficulties of the position, partly because she naturally relied upon him. That position, trying to her, was pleasurable enough to Geoffrey, but he was too loyal to prolong it.

'I was told to look for the Tump,' he said. 'Other landmarks were the Castle and Moonlight Firs. I think I should know the Tump, or the Castle, but cannot see either. Can you recognise Moonlight Firs?'

'Every hill seems to have a Folly,' she said, looking round. 'I mean a clump of trees on the top. Yes' – after a second searching gaze – 'I believe that must be the Firs; it is larger than the rest.'

He took Kitty's bridle, and led the chestnut in the direction of the copse. The distance was increased by the undulation of the ground, but in twenty minutes it grew more distinct.

'Yes, I am sure it is Moonlight Firs,' she said hopefully. 'We shall find the track there.'

Night

Kitty laboured up the steep slope wearily; Geoffrey patted and encouraged the mare.

'But what trees are these?' said Margaret, with a sudden change of tone as they reached the summit.

'I am afraid they are beeches,' said he. He ran forward, and found that they were.

There were no firs. Margaret's heart sank; the disappointment was very great.

'Look once more,' he said. 'From this height there is a better view. See, there are three copses round us; is either like the Firs?'

'They are all just alike,' she said, in a troubled tone; then pleadingly, 'Geoffrey – *think*.'

'There are the stars still,' he said.

'Ah, yes,' eagerly, and looking up. 'I know the north star; there it is,' pointing to the faint sparkle that has been the lamp of hope to so many weary hearts on foaming ocean and trackless plain. 'And the Great Bear; the men call it Dick and His Team; it shines every night opposite my window, over the dovecot. Why, of course, all we have to do is to turn our backs to it, and ride straight to Greene Ferne.'

'Not quite, I fear,' smiling at her impetuosity, for she was turning Kitty's head. 'You see we should start from a different base, and our straight line might be projected for eternity before it came to your window.'

'Then what's the use of astronomy?' said Margaret promptly.

'Well – really' – puzzled to give a direct reply, 'the difficulty is the longitude. But tell me, are there any roads crossing the Downs?'

'One or two, I think.'

'Then we will go towards the north star; that will at least keep us in a straight line, and prevent us from going round in a circle. Sooner or later we must cross a road.'

'Is that all the stars can do for us?'

'Under present circumstances – yes.'

They descended the slope; on the level ground he began to run, urging the tired mare to trot.

'Do not do that,' she said; 'you will be quite knocked up.'

'I do not mind in the least – for your sake. It is getting late, and we must hasten.'

He was now seriously anxious, for her sake, to seek a road, and pushed on as hard as he could. The mare, however, walked up the next rise; at the summit, Margaret pointed to the east.

'The clouds are coming up,' she said. Low down was a dark bank – a thicker night – rising swiftly, blotting out the stars one by one. Another burst forwards, and another walk, as Geoffrey began to feel the exertion.

The 'messengers' – small detached clouds, that precede the rest – were already passing overhead. The white glow on the northern horizon, indicating the position of the summer sun just beneath, was covered. On three sides the edges of the cloud rose up and began to meet above. 'I trust it will not rain,' thought Geoffrey.

'It is getting still warmer,' said Margaret presently; 'the Great Bear is hidden now.' Under the mass of vapour the temperature, warm before, became sultry and oppressive.

'Stand up!' said Geoffrey sharply to the mare, as they descended a steeper slope, and she stumbled. Then to Margaret, 'The mist is gone.' It had insensibly disappeared as the clouds came over; they had now covered the sky, and it was dark.

'Will it thunder?' she asked anxiously. 'It is very hot, and I believe I felt a drop of rain – and another.'

'Only heat-drops,' said Geoffrey, but his mind misgave him. The clouds swept over at a rapid pace, yet there was no breeze; they were carried on an aerial current far above the earth. The pole star was hidden; still Geoffrey kept on walking as fast as he could, trying to keep a straight line. He spoke to and cheered the mare frequently; she stumbled, and seemed nervous. There was an intense electrical tension in the atmosphere.

'Oh, where are we now?' said Margaret, as Kitty's knees rustled against something, and she stopped and dragged at the bridle. 'What is this?'

In the gloom a white shimmering surface stretched out.

Night

'A wheat field,' said Geoffrey; 'we must go round it.' Kitty resisted, wanting to nibble at the succulent stalks, not yet dried into straw by the sun.

'If it is wheat we are certainly wrong,' said Margaret. 'We ought not to get on the plain among the ploughed fields; our proper road is on the turf somewhere. Pluck me a wheat-ear, please; the stalk is sweet, and I am thirsty.'

He did so. Crushed by the teeth, the stalk yielded a pleasant sweetness to the parched mouth. 'It is the wine of the corn,' she said. He wanted to lead the mare round the field; but beyond was another of barley, and Margaret was so certain that it was the wrong direction that he gave it up, and felt his way back to the hill as he thought. Proceeding along the ridge, a clump of trees loomed large close at hand.

'Moonlight Firs!' cried Margaret joyfully, urging the mare. 'Please go and see what trees they are,' she said. 'It is difficult to distinguish.'

He ran forward, and in two minutes returned, silent. 'Yes?' she said impatiently.

'Beeches,' he replied; 'the same beeches.'

'We have toiled round in a circle. What shall we do? – now we are lost indeed!' Her voice went straight to his heart, and roused him to fresh exertions.

'It is strange that we see no lights,' he said; 'there must be farmhouses or cottages somewhere.'

'They all go to bed by daylight in summer – to save candles. Do let us go on – somewhere.' He easily understood her nervous desire to move. The darkness seemed to increase; but he led the mare slowly. Every now and then a lark rose from the turf – they could not see, but heard the wings – and fluttered away into the gloom.

'Hush!' whispered Margaret suddenly. 'What was that? I thought I heard footsteps.'

'It was nothing,' said he, peering into the darkness. He had himself heard steps distinctly, but he would not let her be alarmed if he could help it.

'There!' she caught fast hold of his arm and drew him close. The heavy steps were distinctly audible for a moment, and then stopped.

Greene Ferne Farm

'Who goes there?' shouted Geoffrey, startling her with the sudden noise. His voice sounded hollow and dead in the vastness of the mighty hills. They listened: no answer.

'Let us go on quick,' she said. Kitty moved again, painfully; her rider glanced back.

'I am sure I saw something far off moving,' she whispered.

'Nothing but a hawthorn bush,' said Geoffrey; yet he had himself discerned a shadowy something. Margaret had heard of the shepherds' stories of the weird shapes that haunted the desolate places on the Downs. Kitty, obeying her impulse, pushed on more rapidly; when they looked back again there was nothing. But almost suddenly the darkness increased; it seemed to thicken and fall on them. In a few moments it was so intensely black that they could barely see each other. With it came a strange sense of oppression – a difficulty of breathing. Her hand on his shoulder trembled; even the man felt a sense of something unusual, bent his brow, and steeled himself to meet it. With her other hand she covered her face. In that pitch-black darkness, that almost sulphurous air, it seemed as if a thunderbolt must fall. The mare stood still.

In a minute there came a rushing sound – a rumbling of the ground; it swept by on their left at a short distance. A faint 'baa' told what it was. 'A flock of sheep,' said Geoffrey. 'They have leapt the hurdles.'

'They always do when the clouds come down,' said Margaret, recollecting what the shepherds said. 'It will thunder.'

But it did not. The noise of the frightened flock grew less as they raced headlong away. Shortly afterwards the extreme blackness lifted a little. Presently something like a copse came indistinctly into view ahead. This roused Margaret's fainting hope; it might be Moonlight Firs, and they advanced again slowly. After a short while Kitty stood stock-still and would not move, neither for word nor blow; she backed instead.

'There must be something there,' said Geoffrey, leaving the bridle and walking forward. His feet caught in some bushy heath; he went on his knees and felt. In a yard his

Night

hand slipped into space – there was a chasm; he drew it back, then put his hand again and took up some earth from the side. It was white; then, dimly, he saw a white wall as it were beneath. An old chalk-quarry. 'Thank Heaven for Kitty's instinct!' he muttered. 'We should have walked into it.' He did not tell Margaret that it was a quarry; he said it was a steep place. She wanted to go on to the copse; with regret he noticed the weariness of her voice; she was tired. He led Kitty far on one side of the quarry, giving it a wide berth, and taking the line of the sheep, who had avoided the precipice more by luck than any sense they possess in that way. The extreme darkness had now passed; but the clouds remained, and it was gloomy. He walked slowly, thinking now of possible flint-pits. Suddenly Margaret drew rein, and slipped out of the saddle.

'I can't ride any longer,' she said. 'I am so tired; let me walk.'

She took his arm; in a few minutes she began to lean heavily upon it. With the other hand he upheld the mare; thus the woman and the animal relied upon the man. But Margaret's spirit was unbroken – she walked as fast as she could.

'Ah, this is not the Firs either!' she cried, as they reached some low underwood – nut-tree and hawthorn and thick bramble, overtopped by some stunted beeches, with but two or three firs among them. Passing round the small copse they came to an opening, and in the dimness saw some large grey stones inside. Utterly wearied and disappointed she left his arm, sat down on the soft turf, and leaned against a boulder. He looked closer.

'There is a dolmen under the trees,' he said. 'Margaret dear, have you ever heard of this place?'

'These are Grey Wethers,' she said, in a low tone. 'And no doubt what you call the dolmen is the Cave.'

'Then you know where we are?'

'Oh, no; just the reverse. I have only heard people talk of it; I have never been here before; all I know is we must have been going right away from Millbourne, just the opposite direction.'

'Do not trouble, dear; it seems a little lighter. Stay here while I go out of the copse and look round.'

'You will not go far away?' She could not help saying it.

'No, indeed I will not.'

He went out some thirty yards, and then stopped, finding the ground began to decline. As she sat on the turf she could see his form against the sky; it was certainly lighter. In a rude circle the great grey boulders crouched around her; just opposite was the dolmen. It was built of three large flat stones set on edge, forming the walls, and over these an immense flat one – the table-stone – made the roof, which sloped slightly aside. A dwarf house, of Cyclopaean masonry; a house of a single chamber, the chamber of the dead. The place, she had heard, was the sepulchre of an ancient king – of a nameless hero. This Cave, as the shepherds called it, was a tomb. They had a dim tradition of the spirits haunting such magic circles of the Past. A sense of loneliness came over her – the silence of the vast expanse around weighed upon her; an unwonted nervousness took possession of her, as it naturally might in that dreary gloom. She tried to smile at herself, and yet put out her hand, and touched the mare's neck – she was grazing near: it was companionship.

'Margaret!' Her name startled her in the oppressive stillness; she was glad to rise and go to him, away from that shadowy place.

'The clouds are breaking fast,' he said. 'It will not rain; I am going to light a fire.'

'A fire! Why, it is too warm now.'

'Not for heat, but as a beacon. Some shepherd may see it, and come to us.'

'Indeed he would not' – a little petulantly, for she was overtired. 'He would be afraid, and say it was Jack o' the Lanthorn.'

'Well, I will try; possibly a farmer may see it.'

'But where is your fuel? You cannot see to pick up sticks in the copse.'

'I stumbled on two hurdles just now; one has been thatched with straw.'

'I know; that is what the shepherds prop up with a stake, and sit behind as a shelter from the wind.'

'And the furze-bush here will burn.' She watched him tear some leaves out of his pocket-book, and place the fragments under the furze; then he added a little straw from the thatched hurdle, and a handful of dry grass.

'The stars are coming out again,' said Margaret, looking round; 'and what is that glow of light yonder?' There was a white reflection above the eastern horizon where she pointed.

'It must be the moon rising,' he said, and applied a match to his bonfire. A blue tongue of flame curled upwards, an odour of smoke arose, and then a sharp crackling, and a sudden heat, that forced them to stand away. The bush burned fiercely, hissing and crackling as the fibres of the green wood and the pointed needles shrivelled up. By the light of the tawny flames he now saw the weary expression of her face; she must rest somewhere and somehow.

'Quick, Geoffrey! it is going out; throw your hurdles on.'

'On second thoughts I will not burn the hurdles.' Nothing flares so swiftly or sinks so soon as furze; in a few minutes the beacon was out.

'I must rest,' she said, and went back to the trees and sat on a boulder. Opposite, the pale glow in the east shot up into the sky; as it rose it became thinner and diffused. Slowly the waning moon came up over the ridge of a distant hill, whose top was brought out by the light behind it, as a well-defined black line against the sky. Vast shadows swept along and filled the narrow vales – dark as the abyss of space; the slopes that faced eastwards shone with a faint grey. The distorted gibbous disk lifted itself above the edge – red as ruddle and enlarged by the refraction: a giant coppery moon, weird and magical. The forked branches of a tree on the hill stretched upwards across it, like the black arms of some gibbering demon.

'Look round once more,' he said, as the disk cleared the ridge. 'Perhaps you may recognise some landmark, and I will run and bring assistance.'

'And leave me here alone!' reproachfully.

'No, I will never leave you.' There was an intense pleasure in feeling how thoroughly she relied upon him. They went outside the copse and looked round. The dim moonlight was even more indefinite than the former mist and starlight. She saw nothing but hills, grey where the moonbeams touched them, black elsewhere; great cavernous coombes; behind them a shadowy plain. Here and there a hawthorn-bush, fantastic in the faint light. It seemed as if a lengthened gaze might perhaps distinguish strange shapes flickering to and fro in the mystic waste.

'I see nothing but hills,' she said. 'I do not like to look; let us go back to the trees.'

She sat down again on the sunken boulder, where only a part of the space around and its spectral shadows was visible.

'I feel so sleepy,' she said. Doubtless the warmth made her drowsy as well as wearyful. 'I think I shall lie down.' She sat on the sward and leaned against the stone; Geoffrey felt the short grass, it was perfectly dry.

'If only I had something to wrap round you!' he said. 'How foolish I have been! Mr. Fisher's rug that was strapped on my horse would have been the very thing! I am so angry with myself – I ought to have thought of it.'

'But how could you anticipate?'

'At least, wrap your handkerchief about your neck.'

'I do not want it; it is too warm. But I will, as you wish me to.'

An idea suddenly occurred to him; he went on his knees and crawled right under the table-stone of the dolmen – into the tomb. She watched him with a sleepy horror of the place. In a minute he emerged triumphant.

'I have found it – this is it. It is a house built on purpose for you.'

'Oh, I hope not,' shuddering; 'though, of course, we must all die.'

'Why – what do you mean?'

'That is a tomb.'

'A tomb!' laughing; 'oh, yes, perhaps it was once, two thousand years ago, before Pisces became Aries.'

'I do not understand,' petulantly. 'Do let me sleep.'

Night

'I mean before the precession of the equinoxes had changed the position of the stars; it was so very long ago – '
'Please don't talk to me.'
'But I want you to come in here.'
'In there! Impossible!'
'But do, Margaret; it is quite empty; only like a room. The ground inside is as dry as a floor, and the roof will shelter you from the night air, and, perhaps, save you from illness.'
'I couldn't – no; please.'
'Well, just come and look.'
'I won't – there!' quite decidedly.
'Margaret!'
He took her arm; notwithstanding her declaration, she rose and followed him. She did not resent his making her do it in that wild and desolate place; had he tried to compel her in civilisation, he would have failed. Once inside it, the Cave was not at all dreadful; she could sit upright, and, as he said, it was merely a chamber, open on one side. He then went to fetch the hurdles to make her a rough couch – it was with some thought of this that he had not burned them – knowing anything between the sleeper and the bare ground will prevent stiffness or chill. He saw that the moon had illuminated a valley on the right hand, and walked to the edge, thinking that perhaps a cottage might be in the hollow. There was nothing, but this caused him to be a little longer gone. Now Margaret was just in that state between waking and sleeping when shadows take shape and the silence speaks, nor could she forget that the Cave had once been a tomb. She looked out and involuntarily uttered a cry. Among the boulders stood a shapeless whiteness – a form rather than a thing, in the midst of the circle. She covered her face with her hands. Geoffrey returning heard the cry, and came running.

'What! How fortunate!' he exclaimed. She looked again – it was the grey, Geoffrey's horse; in her nervous dread she had not recognised it in the shadow.

'This is fortunate,' he said, ignoring her alarm. 'The poor fellow must have hobbled after us – perhaps not so very far, as we went round in a circle. Why, this must have been what we heard – the heavy steps, don't you remember? I can make a couch now' – unstrapping the rug, and removing the saddle, and also from Kitty. Then he took the thatched hurdle, and placed it on the floor of the Cave, straw uppermost. It was perfectly clean; the straw bleached white by the wind of the hills. The saddles made a rude support for her shoulders. She stood up, and he wound the rug – which was a large one – about her till she was swathed in it, and a kind of hood came round her head. She reclined upon the hurdle, leaning against the saddles; and lastly, at his wish, adjusted the handkerchief lightly over her face, so that she might breathe easily, and yet so as to keep the night air away. Then he placed the second hurdle, which was not thatched, across the open side of the Cave, partly closing it like a door, but not too completely.

'Why, I am quite comfortable,' she said. 'Only it is too warm.'

'That is a good fault; good-night.'

'Good-night.' A long pause.

'Geoffrey – where are you?'

'Sitting by the door of your chamber.'

'You have been very kind.'

'I have done nothing.'

'You have no shelter; what shall you do?'

'I do not mind in the least; you forget I have been used to the bush.' A second long silence.

'Geoffrey!' very gently.

'I am here, dear.'

'Do not go far away.'

'Rest assured I will not.'

Silence again – this time not broken.

By-and-by he approached and listened; the low regular breathing convinced him that she slept at last. 'She must be very, very weary,' he thought, 'and I – ' Scarce a word had been said that might not have been uttered before the world, and yet he felt a secret assurance that her heart was turning towards him.

CHAPTER VII

DAWN

WHEN GEOFFREY felt certain that she was sleeping, his next care was to examine the exterior of the Cave, thinking that there might probably be openings between the stones that would admit a draught. The hurdle at the doorway, full of minute interstices, and purposely placed loosely, allowed sufficient air to enter for breathing; what he wished to prevent was a current crossing the chamber, for though warm then, towards the morning the atmosphere is usually cooler. He found that in the course of the centuries the ground had risen materially, so that the floor inside the cave was below the level of the sward without. This partially closed the crevices between the rude slabs, and from the raised turf grasses had grown thickly, and filled the remaining space except in one spot. There the boulder wall, settling under the weight of the capstone, leaned somewhat from the perpendicular and left a wide chink. With his knife he cut a broad sod of turf, and placed if against the aperture, grass side inwards, filling it up completely. Then, stepping lightly that he might not wake her, he sought the

Greene Ferne Farm

horses, and relieved them of their bridles, feeling certain that they would not wander far. A few yards from the copse there was a slight incline of the ground; there he sat down on the sward near enough to hear Margaret in a moment should she call.

Now that his labour was over and the excitement had subsided, even his powerful frame felt the effect of unusual exertion – besides riding, he had run and walked many miles that night. Presently he involuntarily reclined almost at full length, leaning on one arm; his weight crushed a thick bunch of wild thyme that emitted a delicious scent. Tall dry bennets and some low bushy heath grew at his side. On the left hand – eastwards – stood a hawthorn bush; in front – southwards – was a deep coombe, and beyond that a steep Down, towards the top of which grew a few gaunt and scattered firs. As the moon swept slowly higher the pale light fell upon the boulders and the dolmen as it had fallen for so many ages past. The darkness in the deep valley became more intense as the shadow of the hill grew more defined; where the moonlight fell upon the slopes they shone with a greenish-grey reflection, which, when looked at intently, vanished. His dreamy eyes gazed far away over vale and hill, and watched a star low down that, little dimmed by the dull moon, still scintillated; for moonbeams check those bright flashes that sparkle over the sky. The pointed top of a fir upon the ridge hid the star a moment, then passing onward with the firmament it again looked down upon him. With the everlasting hills around, his drowsy mind ran back into the Past, when not only men but gods *and* men played out their passions on those other distant hills that looked on windy Troy. The star, still calmly pursuing its way, seemed a link between then and now, but the hearts that had throbbed with the warm hope of love, where were they? Œnone wandering disconsolate because of Paris in the shady groves of Ida; the zoned Helen with the face –

> that launch'd a thousand ships,
> And burnt the topless towers of Ilium.

The nameless graceful maidens with the many-twinkling feet weaving with their steps, as the ears of corn in the breeze weave mystic measures under the summer sun – whose limbs still seem to move in joyful procession, winding round many an antique vase. Where, too, were they? Where the hope and joy of the early days? And Margaret, beautiful Margaret, slumbering – but living – in the massive tomb, where should she be, and *his* love? His weary head drooped on the pillow of thyme; with a deep-drawn sigh he slept.

The star went on. In the meadows of the vale far away doubtless there were sounds of the night. On the hills it was absolute silence – profound rest. They slept peacefully, and the moon rose to the meridian. The pale white glow on the northern horizon slipped towards the east. After awhile a change came over the night. The hills and coombes became grey and more distinct, the sky lighter, the stars faint, the moon that had been ruddy became yellow, and then almost white.

Yet a little while, and one by one the larks arose from the grass, and first twittering and vibrating their brown wings just above the hawthorn bushes, presently breasted the aerial ascent, and sang at 'Heaven's Gate.'

Geoffrey awoke and leaned upon his arm; his first thought was of Margaret, and he looked towards the copse. All was still; then in the dawn the strangeness of that hoary relic of the past sheltering so lovely a form came, home to him. Next he gazed eastwards.

There a great low bank, a black wall of cloud, was rising rapidly, extending on either hand, growing momentarily broader, darker, threatening to cover the sky. He watched it come up swiftly, and saw that as it neared it became lighter in colour, first grey, then white. It was the morning mist driven along before the breeze, whose breath had not reached him yet. In a few minutes the wall of vapour passed over him as the waters rolled over Pharaoh. A puff of wind blew his hair back from his forehead, then another and another; presently a steady breeze, cool and refreshing. The mist drove rapidly along; after awhile gaps appeared overhead, and through these he saw broad spaces of blue sky, the colour growing and deepening. The gaps widened, the mist became thinner; then this, the first wave of vapour, was gone, creeping up the hillside behind him like the rearguard of an army.

Out from the last fringe of mist shone a great white globe. Like molten silver, glowing with a lusciousness of light, soft and yet brilliant, so large and bright and seemingly so near – but just above the ridge yonder – shining with heavenly splendour in the very dayspring. He knew Eosphoros, the Light-Bringer, the morning star of hope and joy and love, and his heart went out towards the beauty and the glory of it. Under him the broad bosom of the earth seemed to breathe instinct with life, bearing him up, and from the azure ether came the wind, filling his chest with the vigour of the young day.

The azure ether – yes, and more than that! Who that has seen it can forget the wondrous beauty of the summer morning's sky? It is blue – it is sapphire – it is like the eye of a lovely woman. A rich purple shines through it; no painter ever approached the colour of it, no Titian or other, none from the beginning. Not even the golden flesh of Rubens' women, through the veins in whose limbs a sunlight pulses in lieu of blood shining behind the tissues, can equal the hues that glow behind the blue.

The East flamed out at last. Pencilled streaks of cloud high in the dome shone red. An orange light rose up and spread about the horizon, then turned crimson, and the upper edge of the sun's disk lifted itself over the hill. A swift beam of light shot like an arrow towards him, and the hawthorn bush obeyed with instant shadow: it passed beyond him over the green plain, up the ridge and away. The great orb, quivering with golden flames, looked forth upon the world.

He arose and involuntarily walked a few steps towards it, his heart swelling, the inner voice lifted. The larks sang with all their might, the swallows played high overhead. When he turned. Margaret had risen and came to meet him, blushing, and trying in vain to push back her hair, that had become slightly loosened. The breeze revelled in it.

Dawn

'Is it not beautiful?' she said, as they shook hands, looking round. He gazed into her eyes till the fringes drooped and hid them: then he kissed her hand. Her cheeks burned; she withdrew it quickly. 'We must go,' she said, all confused. He would gladly have prolonged that moment, but went loyally to do her bidding. He had no difficulty with the horses, they had wandered but a short distance; the grey's lameness had nearly gone off, probably it would quite when he warmed to his work. They were soon mounted; but then came the old question, which way to ride? Margaret could not recognise any of the hills. Geoffrey decided to ride direct east, towards the sun, thinking that if they kept in one direction they must cross a road presently. They started along the ridge with a deep valley on the right hand, and keeping a sharp look-out in the expectation of seeing a shepherd soon, for Margaret was naturally anxious to get into a civilised locality.

'There is a cloud coming towards us,' she said presently.

Another great wave of vapour was sweeping up, and had already hidden the sun. It crept up the slope of the hill on which they rode like a rising tide – the edge clearly marked – and enveloped them. They went slowly, thinking of flint-pits, and not able to see many yards. Presently the breeze opened a gap overhead, and they were between two huge walls of mist. They drew rein, and in a few minutes the dense white vapour insensibly melted and the sun shone. But then as it rolled away and the ridges of the hills appeared the cloud-like mist visibly undulated about their summits, now rising, now falling, like the vast low waves of the ocean after the wind has sunk. Here and there the mist caught and held the sunlight, and seemed lit up from within; then it disappeared, and the bright spot transferred itself to a distant range. A few more minutes and the breeze carried the vapour away, and they rode forward, and after some distance passed through a forest of furze. A rabbit now and then scampered away, and the stone-chats flew from bush to bush and repeated their short note. Suddenly, in following the narrow winding opening between the furze, the grey snorted and stopped short. Geoffrey looked and saw a labouring man asleep upon the sward, his head pillowed on a small boulder-stone, or sarsen. He called to him, and the man moved and sat up.

'Why!' said Margaret in amazement; 'why, it is our shepherd, Jabez!'

'Eez, miss, it be I,' rubbing his eyes; 'and main stiff I be.'

'How ever did you come here?'

'Where are we?' said Geoffrey. 'What part of the Down is this? Where are Moonlight Firs?'

'Aw, doan'tee caddle me zo, measter.'

'But we want to get home,' said Margaret. 'Now tell us quickly.'

'Be you lost too, miss?' The shepherd to save his life could not have answered a question direct.

'You don't mean that you have been lost, Jabez?'

'I wur last night. I twisted thuck leg.'

'But where are we?'

'Aw, you bean't very fur from th' Warren.'

'Only think,' said Margaret, 'all the while we were close where I started from. If May had known we were on the hills! We had better go to Mr. Fisher's. No one will be about, and I can go home later in the day.'

'Show me the way to the Warren,' said Geoffrey. 'Why don't you get up?'

'I tell ee my leg be twisted. I fell in a vlint-pit.'

'Well, point out the road, and I will return and fetch you.'

'Aw, you must go away on your left, toward thuck Folly – a' be about a mile. It bean't six chain from he to th' waggon ruts as goes to Warren. But if you goes up the hill by the nut copse that'll be sharter. Doan't forget I. Zend Bill wi' the cart.'

By following these directions they found Warren House in about half an hour. Margaret's chief idea in returning there was because at so lonely a place their appearance at that early hour would attract less attention, and because she was hungry and thirsty, and the distance was much less than the ride to Greene Ferne. They could hear the clack of the mill as they approached; at the house, in front the shutters were not yet down, but Margaret, who knew the ways of the place, rode into the courtyard at the back, where was the dairy.

'Good morning, Jenny,' she said. A stout florid woman, who was carrying a bucket of water, looked up, started, and dropped it.

'Lor, miss, how you did froughten I! I be all of a jimmy-swiver,' and she visibly trembled, which was what she meant. Then seeing Geoffrey, she dropped a curtsey and began to wipe her naked arms and hands with her apron.

'I suppose Mr. Fisher is in the barn?' said Margaret, not wishing the inquisitive old man to know the manner of their arrival.

'No, a' bean't up yet, miss. He be mostly about by four or ha'past; but he freggled [fidgeted] hisself auver thuck paason as come a bit ago, and a' be a'bed to marning.'

'Lucky,' said Margaret, dismounting. 'I'll go and wake May.'

She went indoors, knowing the house well.

'I'll put your 'osses in,' said Jenny. 'Our volk be in th' pens, a' reckon.'

'I thought your master was a very aged man,' said Geoffrey, as he went with her to the stable.

'He be nigh handy on a hunderd.'

'Surely he does not rise at four o'clock?'

'Aw, eez a' do though. He be as hardy as a wood-pile toad!'

'Can you tell me where to find a cart? I must go myself and fetch the shepherd,' and he told her briefly how matters stood, trusting in her honest open countenance to keep silence as far as possible. Obviously it was undesirable that the events of the night should be generally known.

'What, Jabez lost!' said she. ''Tis amazin' sure–ly. He said as he could find his way athwert them downs with his head in a sack bag. Wull, to be zure!'

With her aid Geoffrey soon had a cart and cart-horse, and taking with him a bottle of brandy, which May sent down, her kindly heart thinking poor Jabez, with his sprained ankle, would require something, set forth to fetch the shepherd, who was indeed in a 'parlous case.' He found him without difficulty, for Jabez saw him coming, and shouted directions in a voice famous for its power. But getting him into the cart was another thing, and many applications to the bottle were necessary before he was safely up. As they jogged over the hill, Geoffrey inquired how so experienced a man, who could cross the downs with his head in a bag, ever came to get lost.

'Why,' said the shepherd, solemnly shaking his head, 'it wurthe Ould Un hisself, it wur. He led I by th' nause round and round – a' bides in thuck place wur them gurt stwoanes be. Mebbe a' caddled [bothered] you and miss too?'

'Why do you think it was the Dev— , what you call the Old One?'

'Cos 'twur he,' dogmatically. 'Cos Job, he run away, – and nothing but the Ould Un would a'froughtened he.'

'Job?'

'He's my dog. I be as dry as a gicks' – the withered stem of a plant. He took another swig at the bottle, and, much encouraged thereby, lifted up his ditty in praise of shepherding:

> 'The shepherd he stood on the side of the hill,
> And he looked main cold and peaked;
> Says, "If it wurn't for the sheep and the pore shepherd
> The warld would be starved and naked!"'

'You seem tolerably philosophic,' said Geoffrey, 'for a man with a sprained ankle; but you have not told me yet how you got lost.'

'Aw, bailee, thuck thur 'Gustus, sent me to Ilsley market wi' dree score yeows and lambs – zum on um wur doubles as vine as ever you seed – and I wur a coming whoam at night, doantee zee? I never had but one quart anyhow and mebbe a nip a' summat shart. It wur th' Ould Un and no mistake. Fust Job he goes off – drat th' varmint, I'll warm his jacket when a' shows his face agen. I sort of looks about for he, and misses the path, and then I wur took by the nause and drawed round and round!' (With his finger he described circles in the air to illustrate his meaning.) 'Bime-by – whop! I falls into a vlint-pit. The nettles did bite my face terrable! I bided there a main bit and then crawls up to the vuzz [furze]. My droat wur zo thick I couldn't holler; and Lor! how the stars did go spinning round! I seed a fire arter a bit by them stwoanes at th' Cave, and thenks I thuck be He this time, you – '

'So you took us for the Ould Un?'

'Wull, I axes your pardin. A'wuver I couldn't crawl no furder, zo I lays down in the vuzz and thenks a' Jacob and puts my head on a sarsen stwoan – '

'And slept till we found you?'

'Eez; this be featish tackle,' meaning the liquor was good.

'It strikes me,' said Geoffrey, 'the demon that led you astray dwelt in a stone jar, with a wicker-work casing.' After which he suggested to the shepherd the desirability of his remaining silent about the affairs of the night, so far as regarded Margaret and himself, and enforced his argument with the present of half a sovereign. The shepherd's eye glistened at the coin.

'Bless ee,' said he, 'I worked for hur feyther. I sha'n't know nothing, you med be sure.' Shortly after they arrived at Warren House. There Geoffrey found that May had got breakfast ready in the parlour, and was made welcome. Jenny brought in a jug of cream for their tea.

'You can't swing it on your finger,' said Margaret, laughing.

'Our housekeeper,' explained May to Geoffrey, 'I mean Jane, not Jenny, is rather fond of gin, dreadful creature. To get it she has to cross the room in front of grandpa's chair; so to deceive him and make believe there's nothing in it, she swings the jug slowly, on her finger, when it's half full all the while. One day, however, he insisted on smelling the jug.'

They discussed and laughed over Margaret and Geoffrey's adventure on the hills, and it was agreed that every effort should be made to conceal it from all but Mrs. Estcourt. Margaret had lost one of her earrings, but May said the labourers should be told to look for it, and one or other would very likely find it, if it had been dropped in or near the Cave. After breakfast, between six and seven o'clock, when folks in town were just settling into slumber, May sat down to the ancient piano and began to play. It was one of those antique instruments, found in old houses, which shut up and look like a sideboard, of five octaves only, and small keys, yellow from age, upon which they say our grandmothers played with the backs of their hands level with the keyboard, and without dropping a guinea if one was placed on their white knuckles. Through the open window the warm sunlight entered, tinting Margaret's brown hair with gold. There came the odour of many flowers, the hum of bees, and the distant sound of rushing water. It was a joyous hour of youth. May and Margaret sang alternately the beautiful old ballad of which they say Sir Walter Raleigh wrote the antistrophe – the reply to the Passionate Shepherd's desire, 'Come live with me, and be my love!'

May (the Shepherd):

> There will I make thee beds of roses
> With a thousand fragrant posies,
> A cap of flowers, and a kirtle
> Embroidered all with leaves of myrtle.
> A belt of straw and ivy buds,
> With coral clasps and amber studs:
> And if these pleasures may thee move,
> Then live with me, and be my love!

Margaret (the Lady):

> If that the World and Love were young,
> And truth in every shepherd's tongue,
> These pretty pleasures might me move
> To live with thee, and be thy love!

CHAPTER VIII

A-NUTTING

'THISTLEDOWN for thoughts,' said May Fisher, laughing, as she tried to seize the glossy balls floating by on the idle air of the lane.

'Thoughts are of little value, then,' said Felix St. Bees.

'Except to the goldfinches,' said Margaret; 'see how busy they are.'

It was a lovely afternoon: white fleecy clouds lingered in the upper atmosphere, so gauze-like in texture as scarcely to diminish the sun's rays when they passed over. The golden mist of ripe September filled the hollows and hung over the distant ridges, softening with haze the outlines of the hills. The fierce stress of midsummer heat was gone, leaving instead a luxurious warmth that lured them into the fields. Margaret had succeeded in persuading old Andrew Fisher to let May return to Greene Ferne. Rude as he was, Margaret's beauty stirred the expiring spirit of gallantry, and he yielded. Although he would not let May go back at once in her company, he fixed a day for her return. Margaret explained to him that St. Bees did not need his money, having plenty; and the old man – prompted too by avarice – sent a gruff kind of apology, and asked Felix to call again. Felix, however, had had his dignity upset by the blackthorn cudgel hurled at his head, and naturally waited awhile before repeating his visit. Geoffrey still stayed at Thorpe Hall, for the shooting now, and Valentine at Hollyock Cottage. They had all started that afternoon to go a-nutting in Thorpe Wood.

The wood was approached by a winding thick-hedged lane. As they slowly advanced a bevy of goldfinches went before them, rising from the thistles, for they love the seeds in the down, with a 'fink' of remonstrance, settling again to start up once more, and finally, out of patience at the interruption, taking flight to the tall ash-trees, to wait till the intruders had passed on.

'We must have some sticks with crooks to pull the boughs down,' said May, 'or we shall not reach half the nuts.'

So the gentlemen took out their pocket-knives, and searched for suitable sticks. Felix cut one of hazel, twice as long as himself; Valentine another of ash; Geoffrey carelessly slashed off the first willow-bough he came to, and trimmed it.

'Yours will not do,' said Margaret to him. 'The willow is too weak – it will split.'

'Will mine answer?' asked Valentine, showing a stout piece of ash.

'Yes, that is tougher. Why don't you get an ash, Geoffrey?'

'I shall trust in my first choice,' said Geoffrey, just a trifle annoyed even by so slight a matter; for when men's minds are strung with love and jealousy the least thing nettles them.

'I think it will do,' said May, anxious to smooth it over.

As they went on down the lane the blackbirds every now and then sprang from the bushes with a loud cry; the song-thrushes, less wild, sat on the spray till they came close. Stray blue butterflies wandered wonderingly in and out, with a dainty tripping flight – wonderingly, because they had but lately entered to the summer world, and

A-nutting

found so much to see they could not stay long in one place. Bryony leaves, shaped like the shields of ancient Norman knights, trailed a pale buff scarf across the bushes. Bryony berries, some red and some a metallic shining green, clustered in grape-like bunches. Blackberries ripening; haws reddening on the thorn; yellow fronds of brake-fern on the tall stems rising beside the brambles. No sound save the dry grasshoppers singing in the grass, and leaping before their footsteps; and the robin's plaintive notes from the ash. So they went on and into the silence of the wood. The soft warmth brooded over it – the winds were still. High up in the beeches spots of red gold were widening slowly, and the acorns showed thickly on the oaks. Then past narrow 'drives,' or tracks going through the woods, bounded on each side with endless walls of ashpoles with branches of pale green; carpeted with dark green grass and darker moss luxuriating in the dank shade, and roofed with spreading oak-spray. These vistas seemed to lead into unknown depths of forest. They paused and looked down one, feeling an indefinite desire of exploration; and as they looked in the silence a leaf fell, brown and tanned, with a trembling rustle, and they saw its brown oval dot the rank green grass, upon whose blades it was upborne. On again, and out into a broad glade, where the rabbits had been at play, and raced to their hiding-places. Here were clumps of beeches, brown with innumerable nuts; straight-grown Spanish chestnuts, with spiny green balls of fruit; knotted oaks; and tall limes, already yellow and filled by the sunshine with a hazy shimmer of colour. Over the glade a dome of deep-blue sky, and a warm loving sun, whose drowsy shadows lingered and moved slow.

After a while they reached the hazel-bushes, acres upon acres of them; tall straight rods, with tapering upturned branches, whose leaves fell in a shower when the stem was shaken. Nuts are the cunningest of fruit in their manner of growth; outwardly they show a few clusters fairly enough, especially bunches at an almost inaccessible height; when these are gathered, those who are not aware of the ways of the hazel naturally pass on, leaving at least twice as many unseen. The nuts grow under the bough in such a position

Greene Ferne Farm

that, in pulling it down to reach a visible bunch, the very motion of the bough as it bends hides the rest beneath it. These will stay till they drop from the hoods, till, turning to a dark and polished brown, they fall rattling from branch to branch to the earth. There again the dead brown leaves hide them by similarity of colour. So that, to thoroughly strip a hazel bush requires a knowledge of the likely places and the keenest of eyes.

As for May, restless and ever in movement, glinting hither and thither like a sunbeam when the shadows of the branches dance in the breeze, she could never stay long enough to really search the boughs. She went from thicket to thicket, constantly finding one that bore more than that she had just left. This butterfly flight soon carried her away and hid her among the bushes, though her merry laugh came back in answer to Margaret's call. Felix of course was with her.

Like money-getting, nut-gathering grows upon the searcher. When pockets are full and baskets running over, and a heap on the handkerchief spread upon the ground, though the palate is weary with eating, and the arms with working held high above the head, yet still the avarice increases. So Margaret gathered and gathered, and laughed and chatted, and stood on tiptoe, and enjoyed the gipsying. Her hat had fallen back almost upon her shoulder, the impudent snatches of the branches loosened her hair, and the fierce caress of the briars tore her skirt. Her cheek was flushed with the bloom of pure young blood put swiftly in motion by the labour. The grey eyes sparkled, and as she raised her hand the sleeve dropped and gave a glimpse of the white polished wrist glowing among the leaves. The excitement, the *abandon* of the moment, gave another charm to her beauty. It is where the river ripples that the sunbeams glisten, not on the smooth still flow. She felt along the boughs for the cluster, for what the eyes may miss the hand will often discover; she let the boughs spring up a little way without quite releasing them, to look a second time underneath before quitting hold. The heap of nuts grew larger every moment.

A-nutting

Valentine and Geoffrey were there, helping to pull the boughs within reach for her. Without a thought of evil, the very brightness, the carelessness of her enjoyment, raised to a bitter height the smouldering jealousy between them. The smile upon her face when turned towards Geoffrey had the inspiration of love behind it, which he in his rising anger could not see. Towards Valentine it was a smile only, though seemingly as bright; yet he, eager for a sign, interpreted it as something more. She knew that they had been the dearest friends, and in her innocence never dreamed that a smile or a glance could play such havoc with that friendship. Her heart she knew was Geoffrey's – it was the very knowledge of his love that made her so happy that day. But under the nut-tree, and the laugh, and the sunshine, fierce passions were stirring in their hearts. Both were watching eagerly for a chance of speaking to her privately; Valentine, to say words that had long been as it were upon his lips, to ask her to accept him; Geoffrey, full of reproaches, and yet with a guilty sense of lacking trust. When the great bush was stripped to the uttermost as it seemed, Margaret stood back a little distance to view it the better, and see that not one nut had escaped.

'Ah,' she cried, pointing to the topmost bough, 'I can see a splendid cluster. Look, Valentine, there must be five or six nuts in one bunch.' There was a fine and tempting cluster where she pointed, the sunlight shining on it, and one side of the nuts rosy, as if ripened more towards the beams. Geoffrey ran to the bush and seized the strong hazel high up with his willow crook. It was an exceptionally large nut-tree stick, stiff and tall, and scarcely yielded to his first attempt.

'Pull gently,' said Margaret, all intent, 'or you will shake them out, and perhaps lose them.'

'Can you reach them now?' he asked; for as the bough came down he could not see well, being under it.

'Yes; I've got them. O!'

For, as the tips of her fingers touched the nuts, there was the sound of splitting wood, and the cluster flew up to its original height. Geoffrey's willow crook had broken, as she had said it would.

'Here are some,' said Valentine, just behind; secretly glad at Geoffrey's failure. He had gone to an adjacent bush and crooked a laden bough down with his tough ash stick. Margaret turned to go there. Instantly Geoffrey, angry and jealous, sprang at the hazel pole that had baffled him, seized it as far up as possible, and hung with all his weight. It bent; he put his foot against the stole, and with all his great strength wrenched the bough from its juncture. With a loud crack it parted and fell at her feet.

'Now take them,' he said savagely. But the force of the fall had shaken the nuts out and scattered them afar, lost among the grass and leaves.

'What a pity! The bough is spoilt too,' said Margaret. 'Why don't you cut a crook like Valentine's?' She went towards Valentine's bush, somewhat surprised at the vehemence of Geoffrey's manner.

Geoffrey took his knife and ran into the bushes to cut another crook. Hardly had he disappeared in the thickets when he called to her.

'Margaret, Margaret! I have found your glove – you dropped it.'

She went towards the voice; the moment she came near he grasped both her hands tightly. There was no glove, it was a *ruse* to speak to her.

'You seem to prefer *his* society to mine,' he said, in a low, hard tone.

'What *do* you mean?' Her glance and surprised expression reproached him for his harshness. He hated himself for his next words, and yet he uttered them; jealousy is cruel, and drove him on even against his better mind.

'I mean that you play double – first with me and then with *him*.'

Now this was not only positively untrue, but in the worst possible taste; had he been cool he would never have said it; as it was he instantly repented. She stood before him silent, all the blood gone from her cheek in the extremity of her indignation, unable to speak. Then she drew her hands away, and her breath came in short quick sobs.

'No, no, I did not mean it.' He tried to take her hand again, but she fled swiftly among the brake fern and the thickets seeking May. He stood bewildered at his own folly; then his anger was redoubled against Valentine instead of against himself. A minute or two afterwards he heard a slight cry, as if caused by pain, and immediately went towards it, but in a dazed kind of way. Valentine was swifter.

As Margaret ran between the bramble bushes and the nut-tree stoles, winding round the tangled masses of fern, and increasing her pace as the full significance of Geoffrey's insinuation became apparent to her, she was heedless of her footsteps, and so caught her foot in a trailing bine of honeysuckle, and fell on one knee. In falling she instinctively grasped at the nearest bough, and thereby did the mischief; for a briar was twisted round it, and a great hooked thorn ran deep into her thumb. The sharp sudden pain caused her cry. Valentine was at her side in a moment. He saw the thorn, which had broken away from the briar and was fixed in the wound.

'I am so sorry,' he said. 'Let me take it out.'

A tiny red globule of blood oozed from the white and polished skin, contrasting so sweetly in colour that he actually paused half a second to admire before he drew it.

'Quick, please,' she said.

He drew it tenderly, and another larger crimson drop welled up, and stood on the delicate white thumb.

'It is out.'

'You are sure the point is not left in?'

He bent over to examine more carefully. The sunbeams lit up her beautiful hand; temptation overcame him and he kissed it, and the crimson drop stained his lip.

'Sir!' She angrily snatched it away. At the same moment she saw Geoffrey looking through the parted bushes behind Valentine, who did not know he was so near.

'A moment!' cried Valentine, in the flood of his passion. 'Listen. I love – '

But she rushed from him. Valentine followed her. Geoffrey let the bushes come together, and Valentine did not see him. Margaret went towards May's merry laugh, which she could hear not far off.

'May! May!'

'Here I am – by the oak.'

Then Felix, knowing his *tête-à-tête* with May was almost at an end, snatched a kiss.

'I will go up to the mill again,' said he. 'I will succeed this time.'

'Beware of the blackthorn,' laughed May, and was very innocently engaged looking at a sprig of oak with three young acorns on it when Margaret came.

'I am glad I have found you.'

'You have torn your sleeve!'

'In the briars – see my thumb.'

'Aphrodite has pricked her hand instead of her foot this time,' said Felix. 'We shall see a new flower in the spring. Let me bind it up?' and he wrapped May's handkerchief round it. Then Geoffrey and Valentine came, apart and yet together.

'I think it is time to return home,' said May, guessing at once from the expression of their faces and Margaret's manner that something was wrong.

'Yes, I think so too,' said Margaret. 'We have plenty of nuts.'

The joy of the day was over; so easily can a few jarring words cloud the loveliest sky and darken the sweetest landscape. They left the wood and returned to Greene Ferne. As they approached the house a labouring man advanced and spoke to Margaret.

'Be this yourn, miss?' he said, and offered her the lost earring. 'I found un on the Down by the Cave, as you and measter here' (looking at Geoffrey), 'thuck night – '

'Wait a moment,' said Margaret, in confusion, for the night adventure had been carefully kept secret from all but Mrs. Estcourt. 'I will come to you in a moment.'

Valentine heard the man's words, and noted his reference to Geoffrey. Instantly his jealousy was aroused – here was something secret. What had they to do with the Cave at night? Nor was Margaret's halting explanation, that she had dropped it while riding, satisfactory to him. Altogether the situation was constrained. Both Valentine and Geoffrey stayed at the house as late as they could purposely, but neither found an opportunity of speaking alone with Mar-

A-nutting

garet. When they left Greene Ferne the two old friends at once took different roads.

Valentine, walking through the village, ascended a slight hill, and overtook an old woman of the working class, who was groaning and mumbling to herself, and bent almost double under a large bundle of gleanings on her shoulder, and a heavy basket in her hand. As he came up, he good-naturedly took the basket to relieve her, and accommodated his pace to hers.

'You seem to have a heavy load,' he said. In the dusk the old hag either did not recognise him, or perhaps did not care if she did.

'I ain't got half a bundle,' she grunted. 'Thaay won't let a pore old body glean when a-can't rip.'

'Well, it's beautiful weather for the harvest.'

'Aw, eez – the het [heat] makes um giddy: our ould Bill fell down; the gearden be a-spoiling for rain.'

'The farmers pay good wages now, don't they?'

'Um pays what um be obliged to.'

'You have a good landlord here – Squire Thorpe.'

'*He!* Drotted ould skinvlint! You go and look at thaay cottages: thaay be his'n.

The rain comes drough the thatch, and he won't mend it. I be forced to put a umberella auver my bed nights when it rains.'

'At all events, the farmers like him.'

'Do um? Never heard say zo. His rabbits yeats their crops like a flock of sheep.'

'The vicar – Mr. Basil – is kind to the poor, is he not?' asked Valentine, forgetting for the moment his own ill-temper in the old woman's bitterness and abuse of everybody and everything. He was most surprised at her venomous spite against the squire, who he knew was of a kindly disposition. She perfectly hissed at the mention of the vicar.

'Our paason! ould varmint – a' gives all the coals and blankets at Christmas to thaay as goes to church, and narn to thaay as be chapel-volk. What have he done with the widders' money, I wants to knaw?'

'What money was that?'

'Why, that as was left to us widders of this yer parish for ever: you med see it stuck up in the chancel. I never seed none of it, nor anybody else as ever I heard tell on.'

'But you get wine and luxuries, no doubt, when ill?'

'A vine lot; it bean't for such as we.'

'You seem to have some industrious people in the village, however: now, that little grocer's shop where they sell – '

'You means Betsy Warren, what sells tobacco and snuff and lollipops and whipcord. Her buys hares and birds from the poachers – her will get notice to quit zum o' these yer days.'

'But the blacksmith works hard. I always hear his hammer when I go by.'

'What – *he*! The justices fined he a pound a bit ago for fighting Mathew the cobbler. Mathew lives with Thompson's wife – he as was transported for firing Farmer Ruck's rick-barken. That be a vine thing – her be as bad as he.'

'The new school will set you to rights.'

'Aw, will a'? The schoolmaster kissed one of the wenches, and got sent away; but them Timothy wenches bean't no better than um should be.'

'Who's Timothy?'

'Doan't you knaw ould Timothy? He be a mower – a' will drink dree gallons a day. That young Sam'l lodges with he: he be a shepherd, a' be a new chap. I doan't knaw much about he, but I've hearn as a' had six weeks for stealing lambs.'

'H'm!' said Valentine, smiling. 'They all seem a bad lot.'

'Zo um be.'

'But surely Mrs. Estcourt is good to the poor: you don't know anything against her?'

'Aw, doan't I? What be her daughter up to? What wur her a-doing on the Down thuck night with thuck gurt lanky chap from the squire's as goes arter her? Mebbe you knaws un.'

'When was it?' asked Valentine, with sudden interest, all his annoyance and bitterness returning. 'What do you mean?'

'Miss Margaret – a vine miss she be; zo grand. Lord, I minds when farmers' daughters was Molly and Marjory,

A-nutting

and no vine Miss about it. That ould Jane, the housekeeper at Fisher's – warn you knaws her? – her tould zum on um, and zum on um told Mathew, as tould Betsy, as tould I.'

'Told what?' sharply.

'What I ses, to be zure. Miss and he wur out thegither a-main bit thuck night.'

'Tain't no use caddling I – I can't tell ee no more. What, bean't you going to carry that basket no furder?'

For as they reached the top of the hill, Valentine, angry now, handed it back to her; she barely took it, and made no sign of thanks.

'Mebbe you'll give I a bit of snuff?' she said. He gave her a shilling and strode on swiftly, full of furious thoughts, the more so because all these innuendoes afforded nothing by which an open quarrel could be fixed on Geoffrey.

'This is intolerable,' he said to himself, 'that he should make Margaret a common talk among these people. What on earth did the old woman allude to, and how came that earring lost?'

It was a pity that the Down adventure had been kept secret; and yet it was natural enough that it should be. The old woman, as Valentine walked rapidly on in the dusk, put the shilling in her pocket, readjusted her burden, and tottered on, muttering to herself, 'The gurt chattering fool to come a' hindering I!'

CHAPTER IX

GLEANING

ONCE MORE Andrew Fisher, aged ninety years, sat in his beehive chair facing the great western window in Warren House. The sun was sinking, and seemed to hang over the distant vale, towards which the old man's countenance was turned. Once more the sickle had done its work, and the golden grain was garnered. For the shadow of the days had gone forward upon the dial, whose ancient graven circles, dimmed with green rust, timed the equinox and the march of the firmament. The merry barley was laid low; and the acorns – first green, then faintly yellow – were ripening brown in their cups upon the oaks.

On the ledge of the chimney, where the level rays came warmest, and stone and tile radiated heat, the last lingering swallows twittered a long farewell. For the oxen had already felt the drag of the heavy plough. The ivy flowered on the wall, blossoming for winter, and there was a buzz of flies gathering on the pane towards the sun. As a ripe pear that waited but the rude shock of the wind, the full year was bending to its fall. Overhead the rooks were floating idly home down towards Thorpe Wood. The long files of the black army streaked the sky with streaming thousands far as the eye could see, and filled the air with the strange rush and creaking of their wings and the goblin chuckle of the noisy jackdaws. The feathery heads of the reeds by the millpool bowed mournfully; and in the hush of the dying day came the monotonous chaunt of the mill-wheel, ever round and round, without haste and without rest; and with it mingled the sounding rush of the race, of its foam and bubble and spray as of human life.

The sunbeam on the chamber-wall – stained azure and purple by the painted escutcheon of 'Fischere' on the pane – travelled slowly as the sun sank lower. There was a picture almost opposite the beehive chair – a picture old and darkened by the thickening of the oil and varnish. It was the portrait by a rude hand of a sturdy boy in breeches and buckles, and with bare head, fishing in the brook. The portrait was that of Andrew himself in his boyhood, painted to please a doting mother. Was there a tear in his dull eyeball at the thought of her – heartbroken by his evil so many, many weary years ago? Was he wiser, happier, now in the fullness of his days, than when, with peeled white willow wand, a thread and crooked pin, he angled in the bend of the brook where the eddy scooped out a deeper hollow?

'Caer-wit! caer-weet!' It was the call of the partridge yonder, in the mead at the foot of the hill; and a distant answer came from the stubble lower down. Ah, the joy of the brown twist barrel and the eager dogs. His sight is dull and sinews stiff; never again will Andrew Fisher mark a covey down as they skim across the uplands.

The blue-stained sunbeam moved onward, the sun declined, and the wearyful women came homeward from the gleaning and the labour of the field. Their path passed close beneath the great window, and their stooping shadows for a moment shut out the sunshine. Such paths used by the workers, and going right through the grounds of the house, may be found still, where the ancient usage has not yet succumbed to modern privacy, and were once the general custom. It was the season of the harvest, the time of joy and gladness. Do you suppose these women moved in rhythmic measures to Bacchanalian song and pastoral pipe, as the women came home from the field with corn and grape

In Tempé and the dales of Arcady?

Do you suppose their brows were wreathed with the honeysuckle's second autumn bloom, with streaked convolvulus and bronzed ears of wheat?

Their backs were bowed beneath great bundles of gleanings, or faggots of dead sticks carefully sought for fuel, and they carried weary infants, restless and fretful. Their forms had lost all semblance to the graceful curve of woman; their faces were hard, wrinkled, and angular, drawn with pain and labour. Save by their garments none could distinguish them from men. Yet they were not penned in narrow walls, but all things green and lovely were spread around them. The fresh breezes filled their nostrils in the spring with the delicate odour of the flowering beanfield and the clover scent; the very ground was gilded with sunshine beneath their feet. But the magic of it touched them not, for their hearts were pinched with poverty. These are they to whom the old, old promise bears its full significance: 'Come unto Me, all ye that labour and are heavy laden, and I will give you rest.'

They trooped past the window, and saw the old man sitting in his chair; and one said to another, 'Thur be thuck ould varmint. He never done nought all his time, and have got more vittels than a' can yeat. Thaay says a' drinks a' main drop of gin moast days. He wur a bad un, he wur, time ago. What be the matter with thuck dog, you? How he do howl – it sounds main unkid!'

'Come on, you,' said another; 'I be terrable tired, bean't you? Wonder how long it wull be to the Judgment Daay?'

So they went by the window, and each as she passed dropped a lowly curtsey to 'Measter' in the beehive chair. Then at last the great blood-red rim of the sun went down, and a wondrous glory of light rushed over the earth. A fiery blaze surged up into the sky, shooting from the west to the zenith, and thence to the east in the twinkling of an eye; like the glow of a grand aurora, but ninefold more brilliant, a deep-tinted crimson. Men stayed and looked up, amazed at the beauty and the awe of it; for the world was changed, as if it were on fire, and the flames like a flood sweeping up from the western edge. Into the chamber came the reflection – as of the last conflagration that we dare not think of, when the sky shall roll away as parchment – and the place was filled with a luminous glamour. Listen! faintly up from the silence of the ages comes the chaunt of the monks:

>Dies irae, dies illa,
>Solvet saeclum in favilla.

The day of wrath seemed nigh at hand. Away down in the vale, and yonder, over the everlasting hills, flowed the wonder of the light; but the old man's face gave no sign, dazed, maybe, by the grandeur of it.

But Felix St. Bees, riding towards Warren House once more, as he reached the first slopes of the hills, was suddenly bathed in the glory, and drew rein and gazed about him. A dome of fire above reflected by the dull earth – a faint, phosphoric, shimmering rosiness among the grass blades. Upon the margin of the world a thicker vapour swelling upward with a deeper red, as of smoke tinted by the furnace under. On the sunset side of the tree-trunks a streak of crimson, and every leaf gleaming on its shiny smoothness; through the thickets a warm haze pouring, and the whiteness of the road before him reddened, as by the breath of flame. He paused, rapt in the deep marvelling which is prayer, and watched till it passed away. Then he pushed on among the hills.

Coming slowly up a steep ascent, where on the summit, among the thorn thickets and the gnarled ashes, was a little lonely inn, he saw a dozen or more men, labouring hard and shouting by the side of the road. The highway had worn itself a gully or hollow, lessening the pull of the hill somewhat, and leaving a low but steep bank of coarse chalky rubble. On the sward a tinker's donkey was peacefully grazing, heedless of the excitement.

'We've got un!'

'Heave un out, you!'

'Lay on, Jim!'

'Let I try!'

'Peach un up!'

'What is it you are trying to do?' asked Felix, guiding his horse up to the group.

'Aw, I seed his toes a' sticking out,' cried a ploughboy, eager lest his share of the discovery should be forgotten.

'It wur thuck heavy rain as washed the rubble away,' said a man with a leathern apron, doubtless a blacksmith. Nothing ever happens without a blacksmith being in it.

'Mebbe a rabbit a-scratching, doan't ee zee?' said the landlord of the inn, leaning on his spade and wiping his forehead; for much ale is a shortener of the breath.

'Well, but what is it, after all – a treasure?'

'Us doan't 'zactly knaw what it be,' said the man nearest the bank, pausing, after swinging his pickaxe with some effect. 'But us means to zee. Jim, shove thuck pole in.'

Jim picked up a long stout ash-pole, and thrust one end, as directed, into a cavity the pickaxe had made under a large sarsen boulder, the earth above which had been previously dug away.

'Zumbody be buried thur, paason,' said the landlord. 'Mebbe you knaws un? Thur never wur nar a church here as we heard tell on.'

'Hang on, you chaps!' cried the blacksmith, throwing the weight of his body on the pole. The landlord, the ploughboy, and the tinker did the same; Jim and an aged man on the bank heaved at the great stone from above.

'Peach un up!' [i.e. lever it.]

'He be goin'.' Felix saw the boulder move.

'One, two, dree!'

'War out!'

They spread right and left. Felix, who did not for the instant comprehend that 'war out' meant 'clear away,' had much ado to save his horse; for the boulder came with a rush, bringing with it half a ton of rubble, thud on the ground, which trembled.

'Aw, here a' be!'

'This be uz yod!' [head.]

'Warn this be uz chine!' holding up a part of the vertebrae.

'He wur a whopper, you!'

'The gyeaunt Goliar', I'll warn, said the aged man on the bank.

'Don't disturb the skeleton!' cried Felix, anxious to make scientific notes of the interment; whether the grave was 'orientated,' or the knees drawn up to the chin; but in the scramble for the bones his voice was unheeded, and the skeleton was disjointed in an instant. The bones were as light as pith, ready to crumble to pieces and little better than dust, yet still retaining, as it were, a sketch of human shape.

'Drow um in this here,' said the landlord, as the buzz subsided, and holding out a stable-bucket which he had fetched. So skull and femur, radius and ulna – all the relics of poor humanity – were 'chucked' indiscriminately into the stable-bucket.

'A' warn a' wur buried in th' time o' Judges,' said Jim. 'Um set up stwuns for memorials, doan't you mind? Thuck sarsen be all five hunderd weight.'

'Mebbe a' fowght Julius Cæsar,' said the aged man on the bank above, 'I've heard tell as Julius wur a famous hand a' back-swording. You med see as uz skull wur cracked with a pistol-bullet – one of thaay ould vlintlocks – and here be th' trigger-guard.'

From the disturbed earth above he picked up a small crooked piece of brass, which might or might not have been connected with the interment. It passed from hand to hand, till the landlord, rubbing it on his sleeve, found some letters.

'Paason ull tell uz what it means,' said he, giving it to Felix, who spelt out slowly, as he removed the clinging particles of earth,

'G.A.U.D.E.A.M.U.S.'

'What be thuck?'
' "Let us rejoice." '
'Sartinly.'

'My friends,' said Felix solemnly, 'this is a fragment from an ancient Roman trumpet – a trumpet sounding to us from the tomb. Let us rejoice in the certainty of the life to come.'

'I be main dry,' said the blacksmith.

'Mebbe you'll stand us a quart, paason?' said Jim, touching his forelock.

'Will you sell me this little piece of brass?' said Felix.

'Aw, you med take un; he bean't no vallee to we.'

Felix gave them half-a-crown for the relic, and rode on slowly, while the group adjourned to the inn to drink it, leaving the donkey, their tools, and the bucket by the roadside among the thistles.

'I knaws it bean't nothing but the trigger-guard of one of them ould hoss-pistols,' the patriarch persisted, 'them vlint-locks with brass-barrels – I minds um.'

Felix, as he rode away saddened, thought to himself: 'That we should come to this – made in the Divine image, and thrown at last into a stable-bucket! The limbs that bounded over the sward, the nostrils that scented the clover, and the eyes that watched and pondered, perhaps as mine did but now, over the sunset! Ah, the tinker's ass, browsing on the thistles, is thrusting his nose into the bucket, I see, to sniff contemptuously at it! "Let us rejoice" – what a satire – '

'Hi, there! Hoi, you, measter!'

He looked back, saw the landlord panting after him, and drew rein and waited till he came up. What he wanted was to know whether Felix could tell him any further particulars respecting the sudden death of Valentine's dark horse that had taken place very early that morning, during a private trial upon the downs. One of the men at the inn had recognised Felix as a friend of Valentine, and the landlord said everybody about there was so mixed up and interested in the horse that he had made bold to ask. Felix was quite taken by surprise. The news had not reached Greene Ferne when he called; probably Valentine, after the accident, had been too occupied to come down from the training-stables some miles up among the hills.

'What was the cause?' he asked, after explaining that he knew nothing of it.

'A' believe a' broke a blood-vessel. A' wur auver trained, bless ee, and auver rode. Zum thenks it wur done a purpose by thuck black chap, the trainer.'

'Why should you suspect him?'

'Aw, a' be a bad un; a' can't look ee straight in the face; a' sort of slyers [looks askance] at ee. Thur be a main lot of money gone auver thuck job.'

'Well, this is news,' said Felix. 'Good evening.'

The landlord touched his hat, and went back, much delighted to have been the first to tell the 'paason' the story. Felix was much concerned at the event, because he knew that Valentine's disappointment, apart from pecuniary loss, would be extreme; besides which almost all their circle had more or less backed the horse – Geoffrey, Squire Thorpe, and all. He had done his best to persuade them not to bet; but now they had lost he was deeply disturbed. He felt half inclined to turn back, thinking the event would very likely put the irascible old man Fisher into a furious state, as he was believed to have 'invested' largely. These delays, too, had brought on the twilight, and already the new moon was gleaming in the west; but, unwilling to return, he finally resolved to go through with his journey.

When he rode into the outskirts of the little scattered hamlet at the Warren, it was dark, and lights were shining in the cottage-windows. He looked for a boy to hold his horse, but, seeing none, dismounted at the bridge over the millpool, and threw the reins across the palings. As he crossed the bridge, which vibrated beneath him, he saw the stars and crescent-moon reflected in the pool, and heard the rush of the falling water. A dog howled mournfully as he approached the porch, and knocked with the butt of his riding-whip on the door, which stood ajar. There was no answer. He knocked again, and the dog chained in the courtyard set up his woeful howl.

'Be quiet, Jip,' he said. He had heard the name of the dog from May, and love remembers trifles. Hearing his voice, the dog howled again, and another at a distance caught up and prolonged the cry.

'This is a dismal place,' he thought. 'No wonder May prefers to be with Margaret. How gloomy the shadowy hill looks, and the black mass of the mill yonder, and the tall trees over the white ricks!' He knocked a third time, and his blow echoed in the hall. 'They must be out,' he thought, giving the heavy door, studded with broad-headed nails, a push. It creaked like the gate of those dark regions which Dante explored, and swung' slowly back. He listened on the threshold; there was no sound save the ponderous halting tick of the stair-clock. He called 'Jane!' recollecting the housekeeper's name; his voice wandered in hollow spaces, and was lost. It occurred to him that perhaps she and the servants had taken advantage of the old man's helplessness and May's absence to go out for a gossip, and he became indignant. He stepped into the hall, and felt his way along a stone-paved passage, which he knew led to the great parlour; then reflected that he was intruding, and called again.

'Mr. Fisher!' The words came back to him, distorted by a broken echo from the hall. The dog without howled piteously. Felix, in the dark passage, felt a strange creeping sensation come over him. He shook it off, and groped his way to the door of the parlour. The great apartment was full of shadows, gloomy, cavernous; but a dim light, from the faint glow still lingering in the west and the moon, came through the window enabling him to see the beehive chair, with the back towards him.

'Excuse me, sir; but I could not make any one hear,' he said, advancing. He looked into the hollow recess of the chair, and saw the old man sitting there with the glint of the crescent-moon upon his eyeball.

'I am afraid I have been rude,' he began; but suddenly stopped, stretched forth his arm, and touched the old man's hands, which were folded upon his knee. Cold as a stone – he was dead!

Felix recoiled, awe-struck, shuddering. It was, indeed, a terrible moment in that empty gloomy house; the dog howling; the moonlight glittering on the glassy eye. He was a brave man; he had faced disease and danger in the exercise of his office, yet never before had the presence of death so awed him. The atmosphere of the room suddenly seemed stifling – his first instinct was to get out. He did get

Gleaning

out, and the cool night air in the porch revived him. Then he unchained the dog, who whined and fawned upon him. His natural impulse was to run for assistance; but the thought came to him that perhaps Fisher was not really dead – quick attention might save him, and he possessed considerable medical and surgical skill. He went back to the parlour – the dog sniffed at the threshold, but would not enter. He struck a match, and lit a large wax candle on the mantelpiece. With this he approached the beehive chair, felt the wrist, looked in the face, and knew that Andrew Fisher had gone to his account. On the carpet by his feet was a crumpled piece of pinkish paper. Felix picked it up, and found that the telegram referred to betting transactions. Then he understood that the shock of the loss he had sustained by the death of Valentine's horse had extinguished the flickering light of life in the old man.

Felix took off his hat reverently, went to the great window – unconsciously drawn towards the light – knelt and prayed earnestly. Then he covered the face with a bandana handkerchief which was lying on the knee of the deceased, and asked himself why the countenances of the very aged are so repellent in death, as if they had outlived the hope of immortality. To send for a doctor was evidently useless, nor was there one within several miles, but it was necessary that some one should be called. He went out and walked to the nearest cottage; a shepherd, with a pipe in his mouth, answered the door. It was some time before his slow intellect could grasp the idea.

'Dead! be *he* dead? Missis [to his wife within], missis! The Ould Un have got measter at last.'

'Hush!' said Felix angrily. 'Have you no respect?'

By the light of the candle his wife brought to the door, the man saw it was a clergyman, and asked pardon.

'But nobody won't miss *he*,' he added, nevertheless; and thought Felix, as they walked back to the house, feeling the little piece of brass in his pocket, ' "Let us rejoice" – they are actually glad that he is gone. But how comes it that no one knew of this?'

Fisher had, indeed, been dead many hours. He had been ailing, as aged persons often are, in the fall of the year; but

Greene Ferne Farm

May had not suspected any danger, nor would there have been, in all probability, under ordinary circumstances. Jane, the snuff-taking old hag, whom May so detested, with low cunning kept the event secret from the household, excepting a crony who acted as nurse, and was glad enough to assist in plunder. Jenny, the dairy-maid, was despatched to visit her friends at Millbourne, and a kitchen-maid had a similar permission. They were easily prevented from entering the great parlour by Jane's report that 'Measter be in a passion, and nobody best go a-nigh un!' This was readily believed, as they knew his illness had made him exceptionally snappish. Something very much like this has been practised at the death of greater men than Andrew Fisher – monarchs, if history tell truth, have been robbed before the breath had hardly left their nostrils. So the two old crones ransacked the house undisturbed. They took the heavy seal-ring from his finger – it was of solid gold, weighing three times as much as modern work. From his fob – for to the last he wore breeches and gaiters – they removed his chain and watch, which last, being of ancient make, would have been worth a considerable sum.

'Thur be a chest under uz bed,' said Jane; 'a' be vull of parchmint stuff – I'll warn thur be zum guineas in un. This be the key on him.' The chest was of black oak, rudely carved, and strongly protected by bands of iron. It was completely filled with yellow deeds, leases, &c., going back as far as Elizabeth, but mainly of the eighteenth century. These they scattered over the floor, and, as Jane had anticipated, at the bottom, in one corner, was a large bag of guineas. Then they added the great silver ladle, four heavy silver candlesticks, and a number of teaspoons to their guilty bundle, and chopped the gold handle off a cane with the billhook. With this tool they hacked open an inlaid cabinet, of which they could not find the key; but there was nothing within, except old letters faded from age, and a miniature on enamel – a portrait of May's grandmother.

'Ay, poor theng,' said Jane, 'thuck ould varmint ground the life out of her. A'wuver the picter be zet in gould; we med as well have un.'

'A' wish us could take zum on these yer veather beds,' said the other. 'Couldn't you and I car um zumhow?'

'Us could shove one in a box,' said Jane, 'and tell the miller to zend un in his cart. He wouldn't knaw, doan't ee zee?' They actually carried this idea into execution, and sent the miller's cart off with the feather bed. Probably, in all their days, the two old hags had never so thoroughly enjoyed themselves as when thus turning everything up-side-down, and rioting at their will. It was a curious fact that not for one moment did they reflect that detection must of necessity quickly follow. They had lived all their lives in the narrow boundary of the lonely hill-parish, and the force of habit made all beyond seem so distant that, if they could but once escape out of the hamlet, they did not doubt they would be safe. At last, seeing nothing else they could lay hands on, they came down into the great parlour just before sunset, and heard the tramp of the wearyful women approaching.

'We'd better go now,' said the nurse. 'What had us better do with *he*?' jerking her thumb towards the senseless clay in the beehive chair.

'Aw, thur bean't no call to move un,' said Jane; 'let un bide. Nobody won't knaw as a' be dead vor a day or two. Come on, you' – making for the back-door.

The wearyful women as they passed the window had curtseyed to the dead. The luminous sunset, filling the chamber with its magical glamour, had lit up the cold, drawn features with a rosy glow. But the dimmed eyeball had not seen the flames of that conflagration sweeping up from the west: –

Dies irae, dies illa.

The wrath, long withheld, must come at last.

'I fear there has been robbery here,' said Felix, as, with the shepherd, he re-entered the gloomy house.

'It do seem zo; the things be drowed about mainly. A'wuver it sarves un right.'

'Hush!' said Felix, and thought to himself, 'How terrible it is to be hated even when dead! We will go over the house,' he added aloud, 'and see if anything has been taken.'

In the bedchamber they found ample evidence of looting. Felix, even in his indignation, could not resist his antiquarian tastes. He took up an ancient deed, and while he glanced over it, the shepherd pretended to tie his shoelace, and pocketed a spade-guinea which the crones had dropped on the floor.

'Who is there that could take charge of the place?' asked Felix presently.

'Thur be the bailie.'

'Go and bring him.'

The shepherd went; and Felix, to pass the time, took a book from an old black chest of drawers, with brass rings and lions' heads for handles. It was a small quarto, A.D. 1650, a kind of calendar of astrology, medicine, and agriculture, telling the farmer when the conjunction of the planets was favourable for purchasing stock or sowing seed. When, presently, the bailiff came – a respectable man enough for his station – Felix, in his presence, locked the upper rooms and took the keys with him. Then, leaving the house in the bailiff's charge, he rode through the starlit night, by the lonely highway, homeward.

CHAPTER X

A FRAY

P
UFF-PUFF! puff-puff! hum-m-m! as the flywheel whizzed round with a sudden ease in working.

'I detest these ploughing engines,' said Squire Thorpe, looking over the gate and leaning his arms on it, as country people always do.

'But if the tenants find deep ploughing and manuring better, I suppose that's the point,' said Valentine.

'For the tenant, yes,' said the Squire, as he shouldered his gun and turned away from the gate. 'For *me*, it is another matter. It is a question with me if this deep ploughing will not exhaust the earth.'

'But the artificial manure,' said Valentine, who was inclined to argue with any one.

'Rubbish! Why, it's only used like dust – not an eighth of an inch thick; and they take all that out again quick enough. Then these deep drains; they carry away as much of the richness of the soil as water.'

'You don't think much of unexhausted improvements,' said Geoffrey.

'The greatest nonsense ever talked,' said the Squire, working himself into a temper. 'It's simply a device to suck every atom out of the soil, and leave me as dry as a dead hemlock. What profit do you suppose I get out of the land? I'm pestered to put up cattle-stalls and sheds, to sink wells and rebuild farmhouses, to put in drains – confound the drains! Then I must make reductions because the labourers want higher wages, and take off ten per cent, because the weather's been bad! As if the weather had not always been wrong these three hundred years! I'm perfectly sick of science and superphosphates, shorthorns, and steam-tackle. Then they bring public opinion, forsooth, on me, and say I must disgorge! [Intense disgust.] Disgorge! Let them take the land, and welcome, and give me an equivalent in Consols, I should be twenty times better off. No; I'll be shot if they shall! [With energetic inconsistency.] I would sooner be flayed alive than part with a square inch! I love the land next to my mother! There! But I'll be let alone. I'll plant the whole place with oaks. My woods are the only things that pay me – except the rabbits, and that rascally Guss Basset poaches and nets them by the score. Look out!'

A covey of partridges rose, and Valentine, who was a little in advance, fired both barrels without effect.

'Mark!' said the Squire. 'Gone to the turnips of course, the only place left for the poor things; this short stubble makes them as wild as hawks. Val, your nerves are shaky this afternoon, and, by Jove, that horse dying was enough!'

'My nerves are not at all shaken,' said Valentine, as he reloaded.

He affected a stoical indifference, though really hit hard. His temper had been boiling like molten lead under the surface, and it wanted but little to make him explode. His losses and vexation, his jealousy of Geoffrey, the unfortunate suspicions that had been aroused in his mind about the night on the Downs – all had combined to irritate him to the last degree.

'Well, we've all lost money,' said the Squire; 'and what a terrible thing about poor old Fisher! May will stay at Greene Ferne, I suppose; she can never return alone to that gloomy house. Ah, that's more to my taste' – pointing to a middle-aged labourer who was sowing corn broadcast.

'Now watch his steps; regular as clockwork. See, his hand springs from his hip, and describes an exact segment of a circle – no, a parabola, I suppose – every time, so as to make the seed spread itself equally. That's higher than science – that's art, art handed down these thousand years.'

A man now overtook them with a message from the house: the Squire was wanted about a summons.

'If you cross the turnips,' he said, as he turned to leave them, 'you may find the covey again; and then try the meadows at the edge of the wood; and if you see that rascally Basset at my rabbits, just –' he kicked a clod to pieces illustratively.

The Squire returned homewards; Geoffrey and Valentine entered the turnips, making for the narrow belt of meadow by the wood. It was not a regular shooting expedition: they had simply strolled out for an hour, and were not accompanied by a keeper. The moment the Squire left, the conversation dropped. Valentine was bitter against his old friend: Geoffrey had not forgotten the *contretemps* at the nutting. It had been long before Margaret accepted his protestations of regret for his hasty words. Now no man, who is a man, likes the part of penitence. He considered that Valentine had forced him into that unpleasant position, and his wrath smouldered against him.

After the turnips, they got through a gap into the meadow land, which, being of poor quality, as is often the case near a wood, was dotted with dead thistles, rushes in the hollows, and bunches of tussocky grass. Out from one of these sprang a hare, as nearly as possible midway between them. They both fired – so exactly simultaneously that it sounded as one report; and for the moment neither knew that the other had pulled the trigger. But when they saw what had happened, each turned away from the dead hare – neither would touch it. Each, biassed by previous irritation, accused the other in his mind of taking the shot from him. This little accident added to the sullen bitterness.

They now came to an immense double-mound hedge, into which the spaniels rushed. Valentine took the near side, Geoffrey the off, with the hedge between them. It was

Greene Ferne Farm

so thick neither could see the other; so trifling a circumstance tended to calm the annoyance – out of sight, out of mind. As he followed the edge of the ditch, waiting now and then for the dogs to work the hedge thoroughly, Geoffrey became conscious of the beauty of the warm autumn day.

Puff-puff! puff-puff! hum-m-m! The sound of the distant ploughing engines came humming in the still air. He had noticed previously that his coat-sleeve was flecked with gossamer threads', and now saw that the bushes were white with them. Looking upwards, the atmosphere was full of glistening lines – like the most delicate silk – drooping downwards and shining in the sunlight. As far up as the eye could see, they came showering slowly, noiselessly, down. The surface of the grass was covered with these webs like a broad veil of fragile lace; and his feet, tearing a rent through it, were whitened by the accumulated threads. The rooks rose from the oaks with a lazy cawing, loth to leave the ripening acorns, and settled again when he had passed.

Hum-m-m! hum-m-m!

Under-foot a soft moss, luxuriating in the shade, almost took the place of grass. The hedge itself was like a wood, so wide and thick – full of ashpoles and hawthorn, crab-tree underwood, willow, elder, and blackthorn, and here and there spreading oak trees. It terminated at the wood; and as they approached it the dogs became more busy; for the rabbits were numerous, and the banks were bored with their holes. Geoffrey kept his gun on the hollow of his left arm – ready for a rabbit – with the muzzle towards the hedge.

'Loo! Loo!' cried Valentine, urging the dogs.

Puff-puff! hum-m-m!

Geoffrey, looking intently at the mound, and expecting a rabbit to start every moment, did not notice that a mole had recently thrown up a heap of earth in his path. His foot striking against it caused him to stumble, and, to recover himself, he snatched at a projecting branch of nutwood. A twig, or perhaps his sleeve, touched the trigger of his gun – the muzzle still towards the hedge – and the sudden explosion that followed jerked the gun from his arm to the ground. Like a bullet the cartridge sang through between the ashpoles, and cut a small pendent bough of willow in twain, not two feet in front of Valentine's face.

'By Jove!' he shouted, 'that was meant for me. There!'

Strung up to an unbearable tension by brooding over his losses and disappointment, jealous about Margaret, and now suddenly startled, Valentine lost all control of himself, and, swinging his gun round towards Geoffrey, without putting it to his shoulder, fired.

Geoffrey was in a stooping position, just lifting his gun from the ground, when the shot, fired low, came with a rattle among the crab tree undergrowth. The tough fibres of the wood held and checked it, so that only a few pellets passed by; but one or two of these, though their force was almost spent in penetrating the branches, struck him sharply by the knee with a sudden stinging pain.

'You shot at me!' shouted Geoffrey, now equally excited, and, hardly aware what he was doing, he sprang across the ditch and into the double mound, to get a clearer aim.

Valentine ran quickly down the meadow on his side; then, seeing no other cover, also leapt into the hedge, and they faced each other some thirty yards apart. As usual in double mounds, the growth of underwood was less dense in the middle, so that, though some distance apart, each was dimly visible through the branches. There came a loud report as they fired the remaining barrels almost simultaneously, and a crashing and cracking of splintered wood; but no harm yet, thanks to the crab and stubborn blackthorn. The sulphurous smoke, clinging to the close undergrowth and tall grasses, filled their nostrils with the scent and madness of battle. In his ordinary mood either of these two would have scouted the possibility of such a thing happening; but circumstances suddenly threw them as it were a thousand years back in civilisation on the original savage instincts of man. Had they carried even the muzzle loaders, which take time to ram the charge home, one or other might have paused. Better still if their arms had been the ancient matchlock, with the priming to look to and the match to blow. But these breechloaders, which send forth continuous flame, swift as the lightning, flash on flash, allow not a moment for thought. The 'death and murder of a world,' as Faust said, be on them.

As they jerked out the empty cartridge cases, and thrust in fresh charges, each instinctively moved to the best shelter he could see – Valentine behind the gabions of a great gnarled ash-stole; Geoffrey to the cover of a crooked maple, whose leaves were turning yellow. Red tongues of fire darted forth, scorching the leaves and blackening the branches. Guided by sound and guess rather than sight, they fired vaguely into the thickets. From the oaks of great Thorpe Wood the rooks rose at the din, loudly cawing, high into the air; then in circling sweep they soared and wheeled, black and ominous, a dance of death in the azure beauty of the cloudless sky. The dogs yelped their very loudest, keeping at a distance from the hedgerow; they knew that something was wrong. Fast as the motions of the hand could answer to the eager hate in the heart, volley followed volley, till the heated metal of the barrels could scarcely be touched.

The dun smoke crept along the mound, and slipped with sudden draught into the rabbit-buries, and hung low over the ash-tops. With a hiss and roar and rattle the shot tore its way, biting hungrily at the branches as it passed. The ash-boughs, tough and sinewy, though half-severed, hung together still; the willow split, and let the lead slip through its feeble wood; the hard crab-tree and blackthorn, with fibres torn and jagged, held and stopped it; the briar, with its circular pith, snapped and drooped. Through the broad burdock leaves and hollow hemlock stems and 'gicks' the hasty pellets drilled round holes, or buried themselves in the bark of the larger tree-trunks, some glancing off at a sharp angle like Tyrrell's arrow. The maple, all scored and dotted, and partly stripped of leaves by the leaden shower, gave less cover than the ash-stole; and Geoffrey, with shot-holes in his hat, and the pellets hissing past his ears, yielded ground and retreated, firing as he went. Valentine immediately advanced, and thus, like Indians in the backwoods, they glided from thicket to thicket, from tree to tree, stalking, but shooting wildly, baffled by the branches.

A Fray

In a few minutes Geoffrey came to a great oak, rugged and moss-grown at the roots, which stood near the edge of the ditch that, at the end of the double mound, divided the hedge from the wood. Behind this he took his stand; and Valentine, advancing too rapidly, was stung by a pellet that glanced from a branch and struck his arm. He hastily rushed behind an ash-tree – it was not broad enough to shield him completely; but by its side grew a thicket of bramble and brake fern that helped to hide him from sight. He blazed rapidly at the edge of the oak; in return the shot came rushing through the fern, and scoring the bark of the ash. Suddenly Geoffrey's fire ceased: the next moment Valentine guessed the truth – that his opponent's last cartridge was gone – and surely mad with rage stepped from his cover eager to seize the advantage. At the same moment Geoffrey, saying to himself that he would not die like a dog cowering behind a tree, walked out from the oak and faced his doom.

In that second – in the tenth of a second – he saw the sunbeams glance on the levelled barrel, and behind the twin circular orifices of the muzzle the smoke-blackened, frowning brow of the man who once had loved him.

'Fair play in the army!' shouted a hoarse voice, and a long stick of briar suddenly projected from the fern at Valentine's side fell with a crash upon his barrel. The blow diverted the aim, but the charge exploded. Geoffrey uttered a sharp cry, turned round and put out his hand as if to lean against the oak, and then dropped.

'We used to have fair play in the army,' said Augustus Basset, stepping up from the ditch out of the fern, with a briar in one hand, and a vicious ferret in the other – struggling hard, but dexterously grasped just behind the forelegs, the first finger in front of the legs, so that it could not bite. 'You make a ring, look here!' in his incoherent way.

But Valentine, all aghast with sudden revulsion of feeling, had already rushed to his fallen friend and knelt beside him, feeling a pressure upon his heart and a dizziness of sight. For the blood of life was spouting from the right shoulder, and already the yellow fern and the grey grass were spotted and stained, and the lowly creeping ivy streaked with crimson.

'Speak, Geof, old fellow!' cried Valentine, becoming of a more deadly pallor than the wounded man.

'Plug the hole,' said Augustus, who, though he had never seen service, like most old soldiers had some smattering of surgery. 'You've lost your head. Here, let me. Hold pug;' and he pushed the ferret into Valentine's hands.

Pulling out his handkerchief, none of the cleanest, Augustus pressed it on the wound, and succeeded in reducing the flow of blood. Geoffrey moved, and Valentine, flinging the ferret aside, held him up.

'Speak to me!' he cried.

'Say not a word how it happened,' Geoffrey replied, thinking of Margaret, and became unconscious again.

There was a rustling of branches and a cracking of dead sticks underfoot, and two men in their shirt-sleeves rushed out from the wood,

'By Gaarge, you, Measter Newton, be shot!'

'He won't die', said Augustus, looking up, and apparently quite unconcerned. 'I put my finger in – it hasn't touched the artery; look!' He held out his hands, which were soaking red.

The two strong men turned white with a sudden sickness.

'We thought us hearn a scrame,' one said.

'Make a litter,' said Augustus. 'There, you great odd-me-dods [scarecrows], you don't know what it is! A hand-barrow, then, you gawnies! What are you staring there for? Go and get your hurdles!'

'Zo us wull; come on, Bill!' and away they ran.

'A man's made just like a pig inside,' said Augustus to Valentine, and he proceeded to compare the anatomy to heedless ears. Quite sobered by the shock, Basset was of more use than any of them. Long hardened, and indifferent to all but the immediate gratification of his senses with smoke and beer, Augustus had lost all the finer perceptions, and had become not exactly callous, but unimpressionable. That very condition rendered his aid valuable at such a time. Even now, under the crust of stolidity, there were not wanting some better feelings in this wreck of an educated man. He was faithful to the hand that fed him, i.e. to the Greene Ferne people; Geoffrey had frequently given him tobacco and such trifles, and now he was really anxious to do his best. As it was, he had probably saved Geoffrey's life; for when the last shot was fired, they were so near that the cartridge had only just begun to scatter; had it struck the head or chest with the shot altogether, like a bullet, instant death must have followed. But the blow on the barrel with the stick so far diverted the swift aim of the practised sportsman, that only a part of the charge took effect in the shoulder.

The two men ran as fast as they might across a corner of the wood, crashing through the hazel, and stumbling in their haste as the woodbine caught their heavy shoes. They made straight for a spot about a hundred and fifty yards distant, where on the edge of the meadow-land stood a rude shed, framed of logs and slabs, thatched with flags from the brook, and walled on three sides with hurdles interwoven with straw. By the hut was a pile of ash-poles, dry and hard, cut a winter since in the depths of Thorpe Wood, and drawn out there for better convenience. These men had been at work for some months splitting the poles, shaving and preparing them to be used as wooden hoops for barrels. Geoffrey, on his way from Squire Thorpe's down to Greene Ferne, had frequently passed the hut, and, interested in their work, formed a slight acquaintance with the men. They told him that these ashen hoops, cut from English woods, went in shiploads to Jamaica and other sugar lands, returning round the sugar casks. He in turn had given them cigars, or a couple of rabbits that he had shot; and watching the dexterous way they used their tools, and how cheerfully they worked through rain and shine and thunderstorm, grew to almost envy their content. They had heard the firing as they worked by the hut, and stayed to listen to it. When it suddenly ceased, simultaneously with a sharp cry as of pain, they guessed there had been an accident. Now these rough sons of toil, mindful of his little kindnesses, staying not a moment to inquire how the catastrophe occurred, ran with all their might, tore down the thatched hurdles which formed their walls, and with these, a couple of poles, and their jackets snatched up in a hurry, hastened back to the scene.

On this improvised litter Geoffrey, still insensible, was placed, his head propped up somewhat with their jackets; and then, as they lifted him, the question arose, where should they take him. As he was the Squire's visitor, it seemed proper to carry him there; but Augustus, who had his own private reasons for desiring to avoid the Squire, vehemently insisted that it was all up-hill and through the wood, and much farther than Greene Ferne. Valentine, anxious to get somewhere, and quite beside himself with impatience, begged them to start; so the bearers set out across the corner of the wood for the farm. Basset walked in front, opening a road through the bushes; but the tall dead thistles, swinging back as they hurriedly pushed along, pricked the pale cheek and listless hands of their burden. They emerged from the wood shortly, and crossed the meadow towards the ploughed field.

Augustus, with his hand now on Valentine's shoulder, babbled in his ear, and showed him the briar-stick.

'I was poking a rabbit-bury,' said he, 'when you came along shooting. There ain't no call to say anything to the Squire. See, here's bunnie's fur!' He pointed to the end of the stick, where the sharp curved prickles were left on, having been cut from the other end for ease of handling. To these prickles a little soft fur adhered, together with particles of sand. 'I found him – he's got his head in the bottom of the hole and can't move, and my other pug is at him. He's young, and wants lining. When you came along I got down in the ditch under the fern. But, I say, fair play in the army! If this had been a ground-ash stick' – swishing the briar, which bent easily – 'I should have knocked the gun out of your hands; but this briar plied, don't you see? I must go back for the other ferret presently.'

He ran forward to open the gate of the ploughed field for the bearers, who were now a little way in front.

Puff-puff! puff-puff! hum-m-m! The fly-wheel whirled about, beating the air to musical resonance; the steel sinew of Behemoth stretched across the stubble, dragging the

A Fray

shares remorselessly through tender roots of pimpernel and creeping convolvulus. Hum-m-m!

It was rough travelling over the deep fresh-turned furrows, that exhaled a scent of earth, and their burden was somewhat jolted.

'Hulloa, you! What's up? I say there – you!'

The men with the ploughing engines had espied the litter, and, abandoning operations, came running across the field. Thus, surrounded by an excited group, the wounded man was borne over the lawn at Greene Ferne.

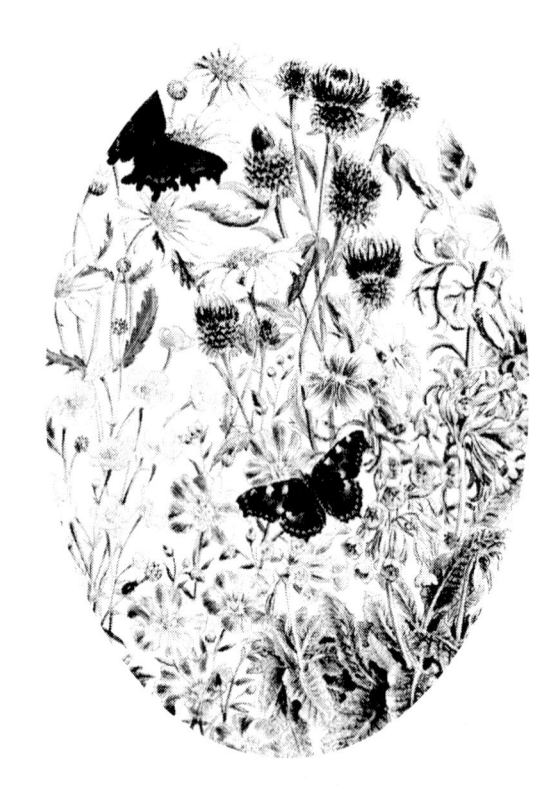

CHAPTER XI

A FEAST – CONCLUSION

IT WAS FORTUNATE that Basset's dislike of meeting Squire Thorpe caused Geoffrey to be conveyed to Greene Ferne, for Felix was there, and he had sufficient knowledge of surgery to staunch the wound. The shock to the household on the arrival of the litter was of course very great. May fainted; Margaret very nearly did the same, but, recovering herself by a strong effort, forced herself to help Felix. The support afforded by her love enabled her to face the sight; but when there was nothing more that she could do, she burst into a flood of tears, yet still refused to leave the room. Felix asked Valentine, who still moved as one dazed, to send Basset, as the best rider, for a doctor from the town. As he got up into the saddle, he asked Valentine if he had any loose silver or a cigar. Valentine mechanically gave him all he had and his cigar-case; and the old trooper, never even in moments of the highest excitement forgetting to take good care of himself, went clattering down the road. The doctor came, examined Felix's work, improved upon it, and pronounced Geoffrey's wound painful rather than dangerous. Augustus, after taking sundry nips of strong liquor with the silver Valentine had given him, in Kingsbury, presently returned to the hamlet, and stopped at the Spotted Cow, where, as he had anticipated, a number of the gossips of the place had assembled. Here he became the hero of the hour, puffing his cigars, and spending his money right royally. But having had lengthened experience of his imaginative powers, they totally refused to believe him now he spoke the truth. They grinned at the idea of Geoffrey and Valentine firing intentionally at each other, and still more ridiculed the embellishment which he added – how he stepped between the levelled guns at the risk of his life. They knew him too well.

'It wur an accident, of course,' they said.

'I tell you they fought a regular battle,' said Augustus, in a towering rage. 'You be a parcel of fools!'

'If they did vite,' said the landlord slowly, 'you med be zure Basset put his yod [head] inside a rabbit-hole vor fear of the shot – and how could he knaw?'

'Ha, ha!' such was the popular verdict.

Geoffrey, so soon as he could speak, declared it an accident, and as such it passed outside Greene Ferne. The only witness indeed was Basset, whose sodden word was not worth taking, even had any stir been made. So soon as the excitement of the day was over, too, Basset – old soldier as he was – seeing which side his bread was buttered, turned round, and openly proclaimed that he was drunk when he made his statement about the fight. In *this* everybody believed him. But Valentine, whose remorse was beyond expression, notwithstanding Geoffrey's wish, gave Felix and Squire Thorpe the true version of the case, laying all the blame upon himself. His jealousy and hatred disappeared, the old friendship returned, and he did all in his power to show it.

Though Margaret did not know all the truth, she was not without a pang of conscience, for she recollected the nutting, and reproached herself for not discouraging Valentine. It was long before Geoffrey recovered; as the doctor had said, the wound, though not dangerous, was painful, and took more time to heal than seemed proportioned to its character. Margaret nursed him with all the devotion of love; May aided her; and indeed his convalescence was almost an idyl. Friends gathered round to cheer and make the time pass happily – Felix, the Squire, Valentine. The two farmers, Ruck and Hedges, dropped in occasionally to inquire. The spring almost came again, before he was strong, and it was then necessary to take a change. The pleasant circle at Greene Ferne was temporarily broken up, but for a short time only. In the summer they met again at the sea, and a double marriage was arranged for the autumn, when May's year of mourning had elapsed. After old Fisher's affairs were investigated, it was found that his loss over the racing was but a few hundreds – quite a small sum in comparison with his fortune. But his soul had become so steeped in avarice that he could not endure it; it had struck him as heavy a blow as if it had been the whole accumulation of his life. There were ample means left – for a farmer, positive wealth – and May was comparatively rich. The old hags who robbed the house escaped punishment, though made to disgorge their plunder. May could not be prevailed upon to prosecute – the whole matter was too painful to be raked up. Basset benefited perhaps as much as any one; Margaret gave him the credit of saving Geoffrey's life, and when she began to show an interest in him the old trooper brightened up. He had hitherto felt himself an outcast. Now he was made much of, the better qualities came out; he furbished himself up, and held his head higher. He could not indeed entirely break from drink, but he did, with an effort, curtail his glasses. He attended to his work, and became a valuable assistant. So much does the mind affect the body, that the influence of kindness can even improve the condition of a drunkard. Valentine, thankful to him for escape from a life-long regret, petted him. Geoffrey, grateful for the blow which had diverted the cartridge, petted him. Squire Thorpe relented, and even gave him permission to shoot in Thorpe Wood. Of this permission Augustus did not make much use. The incitement of poaching was lacking.

 The double marriage – Margaret and Geoffrey, May and Felix – took place early in September at Millbourne Church. As the carriages rolled away, after breakfast, from the porch at Greene Ferne, in the beautiful sunshine, and with the shouts of the villagers and the rattling of rice, Felix thought to himself, 'This day at least we may surely say "GAUDEAMUS" in the fullness of our hearts.' Valentine could not bring himself to be present at the wedding – he would not have been human if he had; but he sent the brides a handsome present each. They are both to reside at Kingsbury, within easy reach of Greene Ferne.

By Margaret's special wish, in the afternoon there was a dinner, or, as the guests persisted in calling it, a supper, to the labourers and their wives in the barn. In superintending this, Mrs. Estcourt found some little relief from the sadness which always weighs upon those left behind after a joyous marriage. It was a large affair, for besides the men employed on Greene Ferne, others working on adjoining farms were bidden to the feast, which was also to be countenanced by many of higher rank.

There was less difficulty in clearing the barn for the purpose, because stores of corn are not now kept. The winnowing machine was stowed away in the corner, together with the polished bushel measure and the broad wooden shovels. A floor so level was easily swept, though the roof was far beyond the reach of the longest broom. It was supported by beams of chestnut – a lofty piece of ancient workmanship, not unlike some noble halls that yet exist. The cobwebs up there had not been disturbed for generations; the bats among the tiles slept on heedless of the stir. A noble apartment it made, wide and long and high; a place where men could breathe and live a larger, if a more rugged, life than in the contracted space of rooms.

Against the door-posts inside, and at intervals around the walls, rose columns of corn; whole sheaves of wheat, stacked in piles, for a less quantity would scarcely have been seen in so great a space. Nor was the white and drooping barley forgotten; and these, the wealth of the cornfields, were strewn in profusion with the flowers that were yet in bloom. Scarlet poppies, blue harebells, the yellow corn marigolds, the mauve mallows, the 'butter and eggs,' and woodbine – all were there, gathered by willing hands. Ferns, some already yellow and some green, tall reeds with beautiful waving heads, and rushes, were placed at the side of the wheat, relieving the bright flowers and the dry-looking corn with their green; branches of oak, upon whose twigs the young acorns were showing; branches of hazel with the nuts, and of hawthorn with the haws, were hung between the sheaves.

The tables, with the exception of one across at the top, were of plank on trestles, and the seats of equally primitive style – stools from the farm, and so on; and when they ran short, a broad plank stretched from one pile of empty cheese-vats to another. Upon the tables, flowers in pots and cut flowers were arranged.

Augustus Basset was of considerable assistance in these preparations – he always was when there was a prospect of unlimited feeding and liquor. Nor did he forget to glance in at the kitchen, and see that the copper was full of potatoes – for no pots could contain the quantity required – and that enough cabbage had been cut to fill a few bushel baskets.

As the time fixed approached the older men began to stroll up, and after them the women – always apart from their husbands; men came with men, and women with women, not together, though they might dwell in the same cottage. Among them were old Gaffer Pistol-legs, Jabez the shepherd, and his nephew, and Jenny the dairy-maid from the Warren, for whom a trap had been specially sent. The men on the farm who, in attendance on the cattle, had been obliged to work till the last moment, now came to the pump in the yard and splashed themselves with much noise, amid the rough jokes of the idlers around.

By-and-by, Squire Thorpe and Mrs. Estcourt, Farmer Ruck and Farmer Hedges, and several more farmers who had been invited came across from the house, and immediately old and young began to take their places. The Squire said the shortest of graces, the covers were lifted, and the smoke and steam from yards of solid beef and mutton rose into the lofty roof. At the cross-table at the top a plentiful supply of game appeared, from Thorpe Wood. Now the solid beef began to gape as slice after slice was cut and piled upon the plates that came faster and faster, till the carvers, standing up to their work, were forced to take off their jackets to have their arms at greater liberty. The

A Feast – Conclusion

clatter of knives and forks reverberated in the hollow barn – the men ate steadily on with a calm persistent thoroughness, like the mill-wheel at the Warren, their chins wagged without haste and without rest. The process was only varied by a momentary pause while the two-pronged forks were stuck into the potatoes in the dish, a much more effectual plan than bothering with a spoon, or while a goodly load of salt was shovelled from the salt-cellar with the tip of the knife. Meantime Augustus, happy as a king, with the can of ale in his hands, went round and round and up and down the long tables, filling the mugs and glasses, never weary of well-doing. No one can understand the latent possibilities of physical development he possesses till he has seen the agricultural labourer eat. It is indeed a goodly spectacle, and for my part I own I love to see it, and wish them all, great and small, plenty wherewith to heartily satisfy those honest appetites. But it is easy to see how we English conquered the world, since

> The seat of empire is the belly.

So steadily went the eating, that before the meat was quite done already the sun began to slope downwards, and shone full in at the open doorway. For the barn having no windows to speak of, the vast broad doors, wider than the gates of Gaza, were thrown open both for light and air. The sunbeams fell full on the face of Gaffer Pistol-legs, who chanced to sit opposite, and lit up his ancient features, which might have been carved by a monk for a gargoyle, so wrinkled were they. After awhile the rays seemed to awaken the patriarch from his munching, and, blinking his eyes, he looked up and placed both his fists upon the table, still holding his knife and fork, the points upward. His neighbours, seeing that the old man was about to speak, stayed with half-open mouths to listen.

'This be the vinest veast, you,' said the Ancient, 'this be the vinest veast, you, as ever I zeed since ould Squire Thorpe – his'n's feyther [nodding his head towards the top of the table] – got up the junketing when the news come of the battle of Waterloo, dree-score year ago. The vinest veast althegither since ould Bony were whopped. Yellucks!' – as much as to say, Look here, that is my dictum.

This poor old man, humble as he was, had many friends, both of his own class and among those above him, to give him a kind word or a lift. A contrast, this, with the ancient and brutal miser Fisher, who had faced that other magnificent sunset on the hills the year before.

After the pudding Squire Thorpe gave the health of the brides and their bridegrooms; and rising *en masse*, they made the old barn ring again with cheering and hammering of the tables. Down fell two of the plank-seats, and added a booming roar to the noise.

Mrs. Estcourt slipped out into the air for a minute, and came through the rick-yard. The rosy light of the setting sun, now behind the trees of Thorpe Wood, lit up the house and the barn and the fields. The call of the partridge, 'Caerwit, caer-wit!' sounded across the stubble. Far away upon the hill shone a brilliant red light – a very beacon – flashing and gleaming. It was the last level rays of the sun reflected from the west window of the church – a light of good omen for those who had therein been made one that day. Yet joying in their joy and hoping their hopes, the tears came fast from her swelling heart. But there arose the tuning of a fiddle – 'turn-turn, tup-tup!' – and her sigh, as she turned away and forced down her feelings, was drowned in a roar and stamping from the barn. It was her own health that they were drinking, and immediately afterwards a crowd began to pour forth from the wide portal. The older men settled to their pipes – an ample supply of long clay pipes, stacked anglewise, was provided for them. But the lissom young men and the giggling girls trooped across the rickyard to the level meadow, which the sheep had cropped close, and which had been also carefully mown for the purpose. Had it rained, there would still have been dancing-room in the barn; but it was warm and dry, so they footed it on the sward.

Mrs. Estcourt, a little shrinking and nervous, had to open it with the Squire; and, instead of finishing, they commenced with 'Sir Roger de Coverley,' that fine old country dance. After a short time she left it, but the rest grew wilder and wilder. The dancing was like a maelstrom, sucking in all that came within its circling sound. Those who had at first held aloof, saying that they were too old or stiff, or didn't know how, by degrees were drawn in, and frisked as merrily as the lads. So the wearyful women, whose hearts had already been made glad, hummed the tune and flung through it with a will. The children set up a dance of their own, joining hands in a ring. 'Let's jine in,' said Farmer Ruck to Farmer Hedges; and away they went with the stream – a sight not to be seen but once in fifty years. The Ancient, Daddy Pistol-legs, sitting in the barn and listening to the music, lifted his oaken staff and beat time upon an empty barrel. So lustily did the village band blow and fiddle that the carthorses in the meadows, who always cock up their ears at the sound of a drum or a trumpet, galloped to and fro with excitement.

The Squire's gamekeeper by-and-by came along, with his gun under his arm, to see the fun, when Augustus Basset, with a fine sense of magnanimity, went up to him with his can and poured him out a foaming mug. But as he went to the house to replenish the can he could not forbear muttering to himself, 'I can't see what *he* wants to show *his* face here for.'

The bats had now left the tiles of the barn, and were wheeling to and fro. But the band blew and fiddled, well refreshed by Augustus's can, and the dancers whirled about yet more fast and furious. Sly couples, however, occasionally slipped aside to do a little courting. Tummas and Rause, after slowly sauntering up the hedgerow, came to a gateway, and, looking through, beheld the broad round face of the full moon placidly shining.

'Aw, thur be the moon, you; a' be as big as a waggon-wheel,' said Tummas, putting his arm as far round her plump waist as it would go.

'Let I bide,' said Rause.

'I wooll kiss ee,' said Tummas sturdily.

'Thee shatn't.'

There was some struggling, but Tummas succeeded with less difficulty than he expected. The damsel was relenting under the influence of long and faithful attentions. Tummas, like a wise man, hit while the iron was hot, and pressed for the publication of the banns.

'Aw,' said Rause, at last, with a finished air of languid weariness, as if quite worn out with importunity, that could not have been much improved on in a drawing-room, 'aw, s'pose us med as well, you. If thee woot do't, *I* can't help it, can ee?'

So the beautiful moonlight streamed down calmly upon the white ricks, the white loaded waggon, and the white stubble on the slightly rising ground. Still the blare of the brass echoed back from the house, the drum boomed, and the fiddle's treble sounded over the mead where white skirts flickered round and round. But the mother's heart, as she stood for a minute alone in her chamber gazing out at the night, was far, far away with her daughter, and almost as much with that other girl who had been to her as a second child.

In the barn the sweet fresh scent of flowers and wheat had long since been overcome by the fumes of tobacco. Big as the barn was, it was full of smoke and the odour of pipes and ale. Hedges and Ruck, not able to do much dancing, had come back, and sat in chairs in the doorway, very happily hobnobbing with Augustus to fill their glasses. At last, however, whether it was the unwonted whirling of the dance, or whether it was the xxxx ale, these two old cronies fell out, and abused each other as only old cronies can, to the intense amusement of the bystanders. These crowded up to listen to their mutual revelations.

'Thee shaved the brook,' said Ruck, shaking his fist. 'Thee scooped out the ground on the Squire's side, wur the bend wur, and put the mud on thy side. I'll warn thee took nigh three lug of land.'

'I only straightened un,' explained Hedges, 'when I cleaned un out. A' wur terrible crooked.'

'Aw! [with scorn]. Thee put all the straightness thee own side a-wuver!'

'Thee bist allus pinching the king's highway,' shouted Hedges, stung by this last taunt, and only withheld from battle by two strong labourers. 'Thee cuts thy hedges by the road inside, and lets um grow out on the green, a-most into the road. A sort of a rolling-fence, doan't ee zee!'

'Beer in, bark out,' said Pistol-legs, sententiously.

The Squire, hearing the noise, came across from the house; and at sight of him the two would-be combatants quieted down; when Augustus thrust a great double-handled mug between them, from which they had to drink in token of restored amity.

'They won't know nothing about it tomorrow morning,' said Augustus, as a man of experience, slightly unsteady on his own legs. 'They'll forget all about it.'

'I thenks it be a-most time to go whoam,' said Pistol-legs, rising with some difficulty. 'Here, Dan'l!' to one of his numerous descendants. 'Let I hould on by thee.'

It was abundantly evident that Pistol-legs was right; it was time to go home. Shortly afterwards the Squire returned again, and announced that the feast was over; when the assembly separated peacefully, after the wont of country-folk, though for half an hour or more there came distant 'Hurrays' and cheering as the groups went down the road.

About two o'clock in the morning, Jabez the shepherd, with his dog Job at his feet, was found astride of a stile in the meadows. He had stuck close to the barrel all day, and was roaring, at the top of a voice accustomed to shout across half a mile of down, the veracious ballad of 'Gaarge Ridler's Oven,' of noted memory:

> 'When I goes dead, as it med hap,
> Why, bury me under the good ale-tap!
> Wi' voulded arms thur let me lie,
> Cheek by jowl my dog and I!'

The Chief Works of Richard Jefferies

The Scarlet Shawl	1874
Restless Human Hearts	1875
World's End	1877
The Gamekeeper at Home	1878
Wild Life in a Southern County	1879
The Amateur Poacher	1879
Greene Ferne Farm	1880
Round About a Great Estate	1880
Hodge and his Masters	1880
Wood Magic	1881
Bevis	1882
Nature Near London	1883
The Story of my Heart	1883
Red Deer	1884
The Life of the Fields	1884
The Dewy Morn	1884
After London	1885
The Open Air	1885
Amaryllis at the Fair	1887
Field and Hedgerow	1889
Toilers of the Field	1892
The Hills and the Vale	1909

Other books by and about Richard Jefferies published by The Richard Jefferies Society

Richardjefferiessociety.co.uk

THE SCARLET SHAWL
Richard Jefferies
ISBN: 978-0-9555874-7-5
Petton Books, 2009

RESTLESS HUMAN HEARTS
Richard Jefferies
ISBN: 978-0-9522813-3-7
Petton Books, 2008

WORLD'S END
Richard Jefferies
ISBN: 978-0-9522813-4-4
Petton Books, 2008

RICHARD JEFFERIES: AN INDEX
Hugoe Matthews & Phyllis Treitel
ISBN: 978-0-9522813-2-0
Petton Books, 2008

THE FORWARD LIFE OF RICHARD JEFFERIES
Hugoe Matthews & Phyllis Treitel
ISBN: 978-0-9522813-0-9
Petton Books, 1994

THE INTERPRETER: A BIOGRAPHY OF RICHARD JEFFERIES
Audrey Smith
ISBN: 978-0-9555874-3-6
Blue Gate Books, 2008